LASSIE

FORBIDDEN VALLEY

LASSIE—originated by MGM
Authorized edition featuring characters
from the LASSIE television program

By
DORIS
SCHROEDER

Illustrated by
HARRY L. TIMMINS

WHITMAN PUBLISHING COMPANY
RACINE, WISCONSIN

"Lassie! Come back! We're not allowed to go down there!"

Timmy tried to stop his golden collie's headlong rush down the hill to the Brunson farm. But Lassie smelled trouble—heard it, too, in the cries of a frightened old man. And trouble was what she found—in *Forbidden Valley*.

First there was the question of who the old man was. Timmy knew that there was an escaped convict hiding out in the neighborhood, and he knew that the old man was terribly afraid of being discovered. Then, with the arrival of the Brunson family at the farm, came more problems. There was Mr. Brunson, who knew little about farming. There was Mrs. Brunson, who wanted to return to the city, and Letty who wanted to stay on the farm forever. Timmy and Lassie were involved in all the troubles in *Forbidden Valley*—especially when Letty disappeared. Before it was over the big collie was to save two lives, and win the title of "Lassie, the Bravest Ever!"

Contents

1
A BIRTHDAY

It had been raining hard during the night, but when Timmy opened one eye to peek out the window, the sun was streaming in so brightly that it made him blink. He sat up in bed, rubbing his eyes hard and wondering sleepily what had made him wake up on this very first day of spring vacation.

Then he heard a scratching at the door and soft little whimpers. Lassie!

Timmy piled out of bed in a hurry and ran to open the door. Sure enough, there she sat waiting, her beautiful plume of a tail waving from side to side.

"Hi!" Timmy gave the handsome collie a hug, and laid

his cheek against her soft white ruff for a moment. "I'm sorry the door was closed. It wasn't supposed to be, but I guess the wind blew it shut last night in the storm."

Lassie touched his cheek with her soft nose, in a most forgiving gesture. Then she picked up a small square package that was lying beside her on the floor in the hallway. It was tied with a red, white, and blue ribbon.

"What's that?" Timmy asked, holding out his hand.

Lassie put the package into his hand, and then barked joyfully, as if to say, "Open it and we'll both have a look!"

Timmy sat down on the floor, staring at the package, his face breaking into a happy grin. He had completely forgotten that today was his birthday! "Golly! Thanks, Lassie! A birthday present!"

It was such a pretty ribbon bow that Timmy hated to untie it. But Lassie kept nudging his hand with her nose. So he carefully untied the bow and set the ribbon aside. But when it came to taking off the wrapping paper, his excitement got the best of him, and he ripped it off in one motion and tossed it aside.

He gasped as he took the cover off the box inside. "Lassie! Look! Mom got it for me! It's a fishing reel! Just like Dad's, only smaller!"

Lassie danced around barking excitedly as Timmy scrambled to his feet and ran out into the hall. Lassie was only a few steps behind him when he dashed into the kitchen where Ruth Martin, his adopted mother, was cooking breakfast.

"Mom! Golly! Thanks a lot! You remembered!" He ran to her, waving the present in his hand.

Ruth turned from the big old cookstove and held out her arms. "Happy birthday, dear!" She caught him in a big hug. "I hope you like it. Dad picked it out because it was the same kind as his, and he heard you say you'd like to have it."

"It's sure swell!" Timmy's eyes danced. "Wait till Boomer gets a look! I bet I catch a real big fish with this!"

Ruth smiled. "I bet you will!"

"Mom!" Timmy was already pulling in a humdinger of a trout, in his lively mind. "How soon can Dad 'tach it to my fishing rod?"

"Why, I think he might manage to do it when he comes in to breakfast. That is, if you're all washed up and ready to have breakfast with him."

"Come on, Lassie!" Timmy ran for the hall door. "I'll be back fast, Mom. Take care of my reel!" Then he was gone, and Ruth heard him run down the hall, Lassie bark-ing at his heels.

Ruth Martin smiled happily at the memory of Timmy's bright face. He had been a timid, strange little six-year-old when he first came to live with them. He had lived in other foster homes since his parents died, and he hadn't expected to find a real home and affection here.

But when they had legally adopted him the first moment it was possible to arrange it, he had blossomed out. Now he was so much a part of their lives and their hearts that it almost seemed as if he had always been with them.

Lassie had had a lot to do with it, Ruth had to admit to herself. It was the gentle, intelligent big collie that had first won the orphan boy's confidence. They were pals after the first minute that they met. And they were always to-gether. Lassie could be counted on to keep her young master out of danger, if not out of mischief!

Uncle Petrie, who was Paul's uncle and lived with them, helping with the chores, had a lot to do with Timmy's happy life there. He was never too busy to stop and chat with the youngster. He had an answer to all Timmy's questions, on everything from planting corn to explaining thunderstorms. And usually he was right.

Timmy thought Uncle Petrie was just about the smartest person in the world, next to Mom and Dad Martin. And certainly the best guitar player. When Uncle Petrie took out his guitar of an evening, and sang "Liza Jane" and "Ol' Dan Tucker" and the other old songs he had learned down along the Mississippi when he was a boy, Timmy could sit quiet as a mouse for as long as Uncle Petrie would keep on singing and playing.

Yes, Timmy was a happy boy. And they were happy to have him.

The small farm was no rich estate, and it took hard work to keep it going. But the Martins wouldn't have changed it for the biggest ranch in the world if it had meant giving up Timmy.

Ruth had told Timmy this, the day he had come home from school with traces of tears on his cheeks and some of the old fears in his eyes. One of the older boys had jeered at him because he was "only an adopted kid."

She had put her arm around Timmy's thin little shoulders and hugged him tightly, while she reassured him that she and his dad loved him just as much as if he had been their own flesh and blood. "You see, dear," she had gone on gravely, "other folks have to take the children that the good Lord sends them and be satisfied. They can't pick the little boy or girl they'd most like to have in their family, but your dad and I had the chance to choose the one we wanted, out of the whole world. And it was *you!*"

"Golly!" Timmy had breathed, happiness again in his grin. "Wait'll I tell that big guy!"

And there had been no shadow since.

Timmy's best friend, next to Lassie who was special, was Boomer Bates. Whatever mix-ups and mischief Timmy didn't find his way into and out of again, Boomer could be depended on to get them both into. They were almost the same age, within a couple of weeks.

Thinking of some of their pranks, Ruth Martin was chuckling to herself as Paul came in from his barn chores to wash up for breakfast. He saw the birthday present unwrapped on the table. "Ah ha!" he grinned. "I see he found it!"

"You mean *Lassie* found it and took it to him! All I had to do was show it to her and say, 'This is for Timmy!' and she had it and was on her way to wake him up."

"How did he like it?" Paul asked through soapsuds.

"You'll hear any second!" she laughed, as Lassie made a sudden appearance in the hall doorway. "Here's the advance guard coming in to report!"

Lassie said, "Wroof!" and Timmy hurried in, hair and face shining.

"Happy birthday, skipper!" Paul greeted him from the sink, as he finished drying his hands.

Timmy had hurried to the table, and was picking up the fishing reel as if it were solid gold set with diamonds and rubies. "It's just what I wanted, Dad. The very one we saw in Colton's window. You remembered!"

"Sure, son! I didn't dare forget it, after the way you talked about it all afternoon!" Paul's eyes twinkled, and he came to the table and put his arm across Timmy's shoulders.

"Will you 'tach it for me, Dad?" Timmy asked eagerly.

"Right after breakfast!" Paul promised, drawing up his chair. "And I see we're having some special blueberry pancakes today. Your mom is really celebrating!"

"I'll say I am!" Ruth laughed. "My last jar of blueberries! Just to start the birthday right!"

Breakfast was on the table when Uncle Petrie came in. He was holding something behind his back and looking very mysterious.

"Morning, Uncle Petrie!" Timmy stretched his neck to

see what Uncle Petrie was hiding, but Uncle Petrie turned a little, just far enough to keep it out of sight.

"Mornin'," Uncle Petrie answered gruffly, and sat down. He still kept one hand out of range of Timmy's eyes. Timmy waited impatiently as Ruth set a plateful of hot cakes in front of Uncle Petrie. Wasn't Uncle Petrie going to say "Happy Birthday" or something?

"Kinda brisk wind a-blowin' this morning," Uncle Petrie remarked casually. "Whippin' away the tail end of that storm."

"Good weather for plowing," Paul nodded. "We'd better get to work first thing on that west field."

"Got to check the oil first. That plow's been actin' a mite sluggish." Whatever Uncle Petrie had been carrying in his hand, he had put it down on the floor beside him and was picking up his knife and fork. Timmy was beginning to think that it wasn't a birthday present, after all. He felt hurt and disappointed.

"Eat your cakes, son," Ruth smiled.

Timmy lifted his fork toward his mouth, and then put it down. He couldn't stand the suspense any more. "Uncle Petrie," he began in a small voice, "look what Dad just gave me *for my birthday*." He held up the reel.

Uncle Petrie laid aside his knife and fork and looked astonished. "Birthday? You havin' a birthday?" His eyes twinkled mischievously. "Think of that! Why didn't you tell me about it?"

"B-But I did!" Timmy's eyes were wide. "Yesterday— an' the day before! Don't you 'member?"

"Hmm!" Uncle Petrie frowned and pulled at his ear. "Wait now! Seems to me I do remember somebody sayin' somethin' about a birthday."

"It was me! I told you!" Timmy's lower lip quivered. Uncle Petrie, his pal, forgetting! He swallowed hard.

"Oh, yes! Now I rec'lect!" Uncle Petrie nodded and grinned. He reached down beside his chair and came up with the package he had been hiding. It was a small telescope that he had bought over a month ago for this very occasion. "Now I wonder what this thing might be." He shook the package and studied it, while Timmy's eyes grew rounder and rounder. Then Uncle Petrie held out the package to Timmy, across the table. "Maybe you better take a look!"

Timmy gave a delighted chuckle as he reached for it, and started tearing the wrapping paper off it so fast that Paul called out, "Hey, take it easy, butch! It won't melt before you see what it is!" But Paul and Ruth and Uncle Petrie were all smiling happily at Timmy's excitement.

Timmy was speechless for a moment as he gazed on the one other thing besides the reel that he had been longing for. When he found his tongue again, he told Uncle Petrie, who sat beaming at him, "Thanks! Thanks a million, Uncle Petrie! It's sure keen!"

"Now you and I can climb to the top of Old Blue some day soon and see how far you can look with it!" Paul promised.

"Wow!" There was real delight in Timmy's voice. "Now I've got a fishin' reel and a spyglass. I guess there's just about nothin' more I want!"

"Except to finish your breakfast before those hot cakes get cold!" Ruth laughed.

And Timmy, with the fishing reel at one side of his plate and the telescope at the other, managed to eat the cakes in record time. He even finished a small helping of bacon and scrambled eggs to top off the meal, while his dad was attaching the reel to Timmy's small fishing pole.

"Mom!" Timmy's round face was flushed and eager. "Can me an' Boomer go fishin' this morning?"

"Boomer and I, dear," she corrected gently.

"You?" Timmy looked puzzled. "Fishin'?"

Ruth laughed. "No, honey. I meant you should say 'Boomer and I' and not 'me and Boomer.'" Then she glanced over at Paul to see how he felt about Timmy and Boomer going on a fishing expedition—he might have made some plans for Timmy. She caught Paul's eye and lifted one eyebrow questioningly.

Paul smiled and nodded. "I guess there's no reason why they can't go, Ruth. Especially when there's a new fishing reel to try out. And a telescope!"

"Whee! Wait'll Boomer sees them!" Timmy was on his feet, grinning from ear to ear. "Can I go right away?"

"I'd better phone Boomer's mother, so he'll be through his chores when you get there. And there's a little job of feeding the hens here, and some eggs to collect."

"I'll take care of it right off!" Timmy sped toward the door. But quick as he was, Lassie was there before him, barking excitedly and prancing around. Timmy dashed out, with Lassie at his heels, and the screen door slammed. A moment later, Timmy's head popped in again. "I'm sorry, Mom. I didn't mean to let it go so hard!" Then he was gone again, but this time he made sure the door closed softly behind him.

"You'll teach that wild Indian some manners yet!" Uncle Petrie chuckled.

Ruth laughed and went to the telephone. "Good morning, Jenny! How did you like the storm last night?"

That was all Miss Jenny needed. The plump, friendly day operator's voice went on for the next two minutes, while Ruth patiently held onto the phone and waited for her to run down.

"They're off an' runnin' at the fair grounds!" Uncle Petrie imitated the announcer at the race track, in a stage whisper. Paul grinned and winked at him in reply; but Ruth looked reproachful, put her hand over the mouthpiece of the phone, and said, "Sh-h-h!"

Ruth was fond of Miss Jenny. The operator had held the job in Calverton for twenty years, ever since the days when there were only ten or twelve telephones in the whole valley. There were a great many secrets hidden in Miss Jenny's heart, but she never told them. She was no town gossip, and many a lonely soul had poured out confidences to her over the wire that had never been repeated. If Miss Jenny had told some of the things she knew, it would have rocked some of the biggest homes in Calverton. But she didn't. She just chattered and was friendly and helpful, solving prob-

lems or passing along recipes, and everyone liked her.

Boomer's mother, Mrs. Bates, was slow coming to the phone, and when she found out who was at the other end, she exclaimed, "Ruth Martin! I'm glad you called. I was just telling Dr. Wilson that I'd better call you up and warn you!"

Ruth gasped. "The doctor? Warn me of what?"

"Boomer came down with pink spots and a high fever last night, and Doc's quite sure it's the measles. How's your boy? Has he started them yet?" Mrs. Bates rattled off her question.

"Why, no! He seems all right so far! But I'll check him right away!" Ruth told her.

"Those two are always together, so I expect he'll have them any minute," Boomer's mother said cheerfully. "Well, we can talk to each other over the phone, anyhow, for the next few days!"

They chatted a moment more, with Miss Jenny coming in on the line with sympathy and advice, and then Ruth hung up and turned to Paul. "Now it's measles. Had we better keep Timmy home today?"

Timmy and Lassie were coming in with the egg basket, and Timmy heard the end of the question. "Mom!" he stopped in the doorway, looking stricken. "Why?"

Ruth hurried to him and turned him around so that the sunlight fell on his face. There were no pink spots. Her hand went to his forehead. Cool and normal. No fever.

"What's the matter, Mom?"

"Boomer's mother thinks he's coming down with measles. Do you feel all right, dear?" she asked anxiously.

"Why sure!" Timmy's forehead wrinkled. "What's measles?"

"It's a fever. You feel hot and you have to stay in bed for a few days, and you get pink spots all over you."

Timmy looked critically at his bare arms. "I don't have any spots." He sounded a little disappointed.

"You don't have a fever, either." Ruth was relieved. Maybe the measles were going to skip Timmy.

"Do I have to stay home, then?" Timmy looked wistful. Paul and Ruth Martin exchanged questioning looks. Paul frowned. "You don't want to go fishing all by yourself, do you?"

"But I won't be all by myself!" Timmy put his arm around Lassie. "Lassie'll be with me. She loves to fish."

"Well . . ." Paul hesitated.

Uncle Petrie chuckled, as he put on his hat to go out to

the barn. He could tell they were going to say Yes. He knew *he* would have, with those big, pleading eyes turned on him! Uncle Petrie never interfered or gave his opinion unless he was asked for it. He went out whistling, but as he closed the screen door behind him, he heard Paul saying, "Well, I suppose—as long as he hasn't any signs of a fever. . . ." Uncle Petrie went grinning on his way.

Ruth held out only a moment more, then, "All right, Timmy. You may go, but you must promise to be home before the sun's behind the hills. And, Lassie, you take good care of him, do you hear?"

Lassie barked and her plume waved excitedly. Then she took Timmy's sleeve between her teeth and started to pull him toward the door.

"Whoa, girl!" Ruth laughed. "Don't you two want me to fix you a picnic lunch?"

Lassie let go of Timmy's sleeve and went racing to the shelf where Timmy's lunch box was kept. She stretched herself up tall on her hind legs, and plucked the lunch box off the shelf, by its handle. She trotted over to the sink with it and set it up on the drain board where Ruth usually packed Timmy's lunch on school days. Then she backed off, turned and barked loudly at Ruth as if she were saying,

"I've done my part. Now *you* get to work!"

All three of them laughed, and Ruth told Lassie, "Okay! I can take a hint!" And she went over and started fixing up a tasty lunch and putting everything into it that she knew Timmy liked. And she didn't forget a meaty bone for Lassie.

A few minutes later, Paul and Ruth Martin stood in the front yard of the little farmhouse, and watched two figures disappear up the road. Timmy had the fishing pole over one shoulder, and the new telescope clutched in his hand, while Lassie was carrying the lunch box daintily in her teeth as she trotted along beside him.

"I hope he'll be careful," Ruth sighed. "The creek bank may be slippery after last night's storm."

"Don't worry," Paul told her with a smile, "Lassie'll see that nothing happens to him!"

2

FORBIDDEN GROUND

It was pretty close to half a mile from the Martin farm before the woods began. At first, the trees were sort of scattered, and there were a lot of stumps to show where the Calverton settlers had cut the wood for their houses a long time ago. But as Timmy and Lassie made their way deeper into the woods, the trees were thicker, and so close together at some places that it was quite dark under them.

Timmy liked the woods. There were spring violets, blue and white, under the trees, and Johnny-jump-ups with their funny little faces all alike that seemed to be watching you as you walked by. And the new leaves were the prettiest pale green on the bushes and trees. But best of all, it smelled so good. Sort of damp, but sweet. And he could catch glimpses of brown birds flitting between the trees, making busy little twittering noises. Probably building their nests, he thought. Well, he wouldn't climb any trees to bother them. Mom told him how they ate bugs off the vegetables in Dad's truck garden. They were real friends of the farmers.

So he just kept on going toward Willow Creek, and Lassie trotted right along with him, sometimes running ahead and sniffing the ground as if she wanted to be sure there was nothing dangerous waiting for Timmy. Other times, she kept very close to his side, especially when there were little crackling noises in the brush. She was careful to stay between him and the noises, and now and then she would sort of growl under her breath as she stared at the bushes. When she did that, Timmy would swallow hard and hurry a little till they were well past the danger spot. But he never did catch a glimpse of anything except once a gray squirrel scampered up a tree trunk not five feet away, and chattered angrily at both him and Lassie.

Timmy stood still and laughed at the squirrel, and made a noise, "K-k-k-kuk!" at it. The squirrel switched its tail and ran far up the tree and out of sight. Timmy leaned 'way back and stared up, but all he could see in the branches up there was a little patch of leaves moving as if something might have just landed in it. Lassie set down the lunch pail, sat up, and barked at the shaking leaves.

And just as she did, a nut dropped straight down and went *kerplunk!* right on her nose. "Yip!" Lassie shook her head and pawed at her nose.

Timmy glared up indignantly at the unseen attacker, who was chattering loudly again. "That's a mean trick, Mister Bushytail! Lassie was only sayin' hello!" He dropped to his knees beside Lassie, who was still pawing at her nose, as if the nut had stung it badly. "Lemme see, girl!" Timmy gently held her paw aside and took a look at the nose. He couldn't see where the nut had hit. "It looks okay, but I bet it hurts! That ol' squirrel ought t'be ashamed of himself!"

But Lassie seemed to be willing to forget the whole thing now. She stood up and ran to the path through the woods. "Wroof!" She looked back impatiently, as if she were saying, "Let's get out of here before something else happens to us!"

Timmy followed her, with a last reproachful look up at the squirrel, who was now making some loud noises that sounded to Timmy suspiciously like squirrel laughs, if there were such things!

Timmy's favorite fishing spot was in bright sunlight by the time he and Lassie arrived. He had a small can of worms in his pocket for baiting the hook, and he chose the fattest one for his first try. "Got to have a big worm for a big fish," he told Lassie, but Lassie was more interested in trying to catch some very tiny minnows swimming in a little pool filled up by the rain.

Things were very wet, and the creek bank was muddy and slippery. Timmy cast his line well out into the middle of the creek, and a couple of minutes later, the reel was singing as something carried the hook along swiftly through the rain-swollen stream. The rod jerked and bent.

Timmy hung on to the fishing rod and yelled with excitement. When the pull continued, he tried to "play" the unseen fish, and reel it in a little at a time.

Lassie had given up her minnow-chasing and was standing up on the bank, watching as Timmy struggled to pull in his catch. Suddenly Timmy's feet slipped on the muddy slope, and he started to fall backward. The fishing rod was jerked out of his hands by the pull of the rushing creek, and flew out into the middle of the stream.

By the time Timmy had scrambled, mud-caked, to his feet again, the rod and precious reel were out of sight, carried away by the swift current. They came into sight again just once, as the water tossed them against a rock in midstream. Then they were swallowed up.

Timmy didn't stop to think. He started down the bank toward the water, slipping and sliding in the mud. But before he could reach the edge of the creek, Lassie had made a long leap from the top of the bank, and grabbed hold of him by his belt.

Timmy was pulled off his feet, but he tried to scramble up and tear himself loose. "Let go, Lassie! I got to bring back my rod an' reel!" But Lassie held on.

Timmy gave up, and sat down in the mud. He had a hard time fighting back his tears, and Lassie poked a comforting nose against his cheek. Timmy slipped his arm over her neck and rested his head against her white ruff. "Okay, Lassie. I guess you were right. There was no use tryin'. But it was my brand-new birthday present." He choked back a small sob.

Lassie whined sympathetically and they sat leaning against each other for a couple of minutes, both caked with mud.

Timmy sat up straight suddenly, wiped his sleeve across his eyes, and looked scared. "Golly, Lassie! I just thought of somethin'! I'm glad you didn't let me go in the water! I forgot I can't swim!" Lassie barked, and Timmy hugged her and said, "Thanks, Lassie!" She pranced around, while Timmy stood up and tried to brush the sticky mud off his corduroys. But now a brisk spring breeze had come up and was sweeping through the woods and making him shiver.

"Guess we better find some place out of the wind, where I can dry off," he told Lassie, and looked around for it.

His face brightened as he saw the familiar long slope of Old Blue Top, not over a hundred yards away. The sun was beating down on the lush green grass of the hillside, and the breeze up there seemed to be gentler than down in the woods, as it moved the grass in long slow waves. "Come on, Lassie!" He started off, lunch box in one hand and the telescope in his other. "We'll climb to the top an' look down at the haunted house. I bet we'll see lots of things with our new telescope!"

But Lassie stood her ground and barked at him. Timmy went a few feet, and then noticed that she wasn't following.

"I'm not going near the house, honest!" he assured her, impatiently. "I promised Dad I wouldn't, and I'm not going to. So come on. We can look through the spyglass, 'thout breaking our promise!"

Lassie hesitated, her head tilted to one side as if she were thinking it over. She whimpered a little, uneasily.

"Aw, come on!" Timmy urged. *"I'm* goin', anyhow!" And he set out for the hillside. Lassie hesitated for a second till she saw that he was going ahead without her, and then she gave up and went bounding after him.

And for the whole long hike up the slope of Calverton County's longest and tallest hill, she stayed close by her small owner's side, her eyes alert for possible danger, and her sensitive nose sniffing cautiously for threatening scents.

Timmy was tired, but quite dried off by the time they reached the tall old oak tree that topped the hill. An old rail fence marked the boundary of the Brunson farm down in the valley below. Timmy sat down on a flat rock close by the fence and caught his breath, while Lassie stretched out close beside him.

The last time Timmy had been up here was 'way last fall. He and Boomer had been exploring the hill, and had sat down to rest right here. They had been surprised, as they peered down through the old fence, to see a boarded-up house down there, and old weathered farm buildings without a sign of life around them.

Timmy, as a newcomer to Calverton, had no idea whose place it was, but Boomer had. "It's the haunted house!" he had announced, his eyes wide with alarm. "It's got ghosts in it! We better not go any closer!"

"Huh! Mom says there's no such thing. An' anyhow, if any ol' ghosts tried to come after me, I'd punch 'em right in the nose, bang!" Timmy had boasted. But he had been quite willing to run back down the hill to the woods with Boomer.

They hadn't come up here since, because that very afternoon they had discovered a deep cave in a hill down in the very thickest part of the woods. There were all sorts of fascinating things in the cave—part of an old saddle, the remains of a fire covered now with cobwebs, a rusty broken shovel. They had claimed the cave as their very own secret hiding place, and they came to it whenever they could, to sit around and dream up all sorts of things that might have happened in the days of trappers and Indians long ago.

When Timmy had told about seeing the haunted house, his mom and dad had told him that the ghosts were just a make-believe, like Halloween, but they made him promise to stay away from the old farm anyhow. There were pieces of old rusty farm machinery that had stood out in the sun and rain for twenty or more years. A cut from that rusty metal could hurt a lot and be very serious. Also, the Brunsons, who used to live there, were said to have had two wells, and he could easily fall into one of them if he got to running around carelessly.

"Besides," Uncle Petrie had warned Timmy, "if the sheriff comes along and catches you trespassin'—which means bein' where you oughtn't to be—it'll cost your folks a fine. There's signs at both ends of Brunson's valley, warning everybody to stay clear. So better keep away."

So the Brunson homestead, abandoned over twenty years ago, had become a forbidden spot, and Timmy hadn't thought of it for a long time. Now, here he was, with a spyglass he could use to study the old house from a safe distance.

He climbed to the second rail of the old fence, and hooked his leg around the post to steady himself. Then he leaned over so he could get a good look at the whole farmhouse and barn at once. Without Boomer to talk about ghosts flitting around the place, it looked pretty dull and uninteresting.

He took out the spyglass and focused it on the front door

of the house. It was boarded up, just as it had been before. He let the spyglass sweep along the front porch, but there was no sign of life there. He turned it toward the barn, idly. But the big doors were padlocked shut.

The rest of the place seemed to be just as deserted as it had been months ago. Only the tall trees in the yard looked different. Last fall they had been covered with bright red and gold leaves, but today the leaves were pale green and still so tiny that he could look straight through the branches and see into the back yard. But there was nothing interesting to look at.

Timmy put down the spyglass. It was sort of nice to see things bigger through the glass, but when there was nothing special to look at, it didn't seem very exciting.

Lassie saw him start to climb down off the fence, and she barked excitedly, ran over, and picked up the lunch pail by its handle. She couldn't have said it any plainer. She thought it was time for lunch!

"That's a very good idea, Lassie," Timmy agreed, so they sat down in the shade of the oak tree, and had their lunch.

And when Timmy had eaten all he could hold of the delicious sandwiches and the cookies Mom had packed for him, and Lassie had polished up the bone Mom had put in for her, they both stretched out for a nap.

The last thing that Timmy remembered was the low buzzing sound of the bees that were swarming somewhere in the high branches above him. Now and then one of them would buzz past rather close, but Timmy just let him go. He knew if he hit at the bee and scared it, he might get a painful sting. So long as he let it alone, it wouldn't bother him.

But Lassie didn't really fall asleep the way Timmy did. She just lay quiet, on guard, her nose resting lightly on Timmy's ankle.

And after a little while, she lifted her head suddenly, her long silky ears standing straight up, and listened. Deep down in her throat a little growl started softly. She lay quiet another minute, still listening. Then, slowly, she rose to her feet, stood with her head thrown back, and waited for what would happen next.

It was only a faint noise that the big collie had heard, a far-off sound of metal striking a rock. But it was a man-made sound, and it was enough to put her on guard.

Now she moved slowly to the old fence, rose up on her hind legs, and stood with her forefeet on the rail, looking down toward the old farmhouse. And as she stood there, the growl grew louder in her throat, and the hair on the back of her neck rose threateningly.

A shambling figure was crossing the farmyard, a tin bucket swinging from its hand. It was the figure of an old, bearded man in a faded denim suit, and it moved unsteadily toward a rock-rimmed well in the corner of the yard under the maple trees. The well was covered by two heavy planks.

The elderly man set his tin bucket down and struggled with one of the planks, pushing and shoving it to get it clear of the well. It seemed to be almost too much for his strength, but he finally managed to dump it to the ground, out of the way.

He rested a moment, leaning on the rim as if to catch his breath. Then he got the tin bucket and carefully let it down into the well on the end of the rope, leaning far over to watch it.

Up on the hill, Lassie barked suddenly down at the man at the well, and Timmy woke with a start of surprise.

The old man, startled by the loud barking, looked up to see where it was coming from, and the rope slipped through his fingers. He made a wild grab for it, missed, and plunged down, heels over head, into the well. His yell of surprise and alarm ended in a big splash.

Up above, Timmy had heard the yell. He staggered to his feet and started over toward the fence. But Lassie wasn't waiting. In a flash, she was through the fence and running at top speed down the hill toward the farmyard.

"Lassie! Come back! We're not allowed to go down there!"

But Lassie kept right on racing down the hill into the forbidden valley as if she hadn't heard Timmy. It was the first time she hadn't come to him when he called her.

Now Timmy heard the call for help again. He couldn't see anyone below, but he knew that Lassie would find whoever it was in trouble. And maybe he had better see if he could help, too.

He climbed through the fence, and a moment later he was running down the hill after Lassie as fast as he could go, calling, "Wait for me, Lassie! I'm coming, too!"

3

THE STRANGER

The man down in the well gave a last faint shout as Lassie came coursing down the hill and into the weed-grown farmyard. She stopped midway across it, and threw back her head to sniff inquiringly in all directions.

Then she heard a faint scrambling sound from over at the partly covered old well. She ran to investigate.

She jumped onto the rock-set rim and looked down at the stranger who was hanging on with both hands to a jutting stone, eight or nine feet below. He hung half in the water and half out.

While the big collie watched, the man below reached for a higher rock in the wall, to pull himself clear of the water.

But it was wet and slippery, and his hand slid right off it. He fell back into the water with a great splash, and disappeared for a moment. Then he rose sputtering and struggling to reach the rock he had been holding onto at first. When he did catch hold of it, he held on desperately with both hands, panting and gasping.

Lassie barked down sharply at him, and the man looked up hopefully. But when Timmy's round little face appeared suddenly beside Lassie's, the stranger below groaned with disappointment. A small boy and a dog! What could they do? But maybe there was someone else with them!

"Bring somebody to pull me out of here, sonny!" he called up to Timmy. "Hurry! This water's cold!"

"There's nobody around but me an' Lassie!" Timmy told him. "But *we'll* help. What'll we do?"

For a moment, the stranger couldn't think of an answer. Then he gasped, "A rope—there's a long rope—hanging in the barn—right by the side door that's open. Fetch it, and hurry!"

"Right away!" Timmy's face disappeared, and Lassie's with it.

The gray-bearded man, shivering in the icy cold well water, hung onto the wall, but he was getting very tired.

His hands were almost too numb to hold on much longer.

The side door that was open was one that Timmy hadn't been able to see from above. He held back in the doorway and stared into the dark interior. He thought suddenly of what Boomer had told him about the place being haunted. He wasn't quite sure he wanted to go in there.

Something nudged him between the shoulders, and he jumped and said, "Oof!" But when he looked around, it was Lassie. She seemed to be telling him it was all right to go in. And when he still hesitated, she trotted ahead of him, and disappeared into the darkness.

"Sure looks spooky!" Timmy told himself, but he went in. He knew Lassie wouldn't lead him any place where it might be dangerous.

It was hard to see anything in there for a moment, but his eyes soon got used to the dimness, and he saw that it was just an ordinary empty old barn. Sure enough, just a few feet away, hanging on a big nail, was a coil of rope.

Timmy hurried over to it, but it was a foot or two higher than he could reach. He would have to climb onto something to get the rope. But on what? There wasn't a bucket or an old sawhorse, or anything that he could stand on. There wasn't even a stick of wood around that he could use to catch a loop of the rope and pull it down.

He tried jumping and trying to grab the loose end of the rope, but it was just too high. "I guess we can't get it down. We'll have to look for some other rope—or somethin' . . ." he told Lassie. But he didn't see any other rope, and he decided to try one last jump to grab the rope. He missed by a few inches, lost his balance as he came down, tumbled, and landed sprawling.

Lassie had been standing with her head cocked to one side, watching his antics closely. Now she went over to him and nuzzled him, whimpering.

"I'm okay, Lassie," he reassured her. "I was tryin' to pull down that rope," he pointed to it, "but I guess it's no use. We'll have to go back an' tell the man." He began to get to his feet. "C'mon, Lassie."

But Lassie ran over to the wall, leaped high in the air, and grabbed the end of the rope.

"You got it!" Timmy shouted happily, and ran to take it from her. The rope came down easily, loop after loop, and in a minute Timmy and Lassie were running out of the barn, trailing it after them.

"We got the rope!" Timmy called down the well. "What shall I do now?"

"Tie it to the maple tree, and drop me the other end!"

Timmy's knot wasn't very neat, but it held fast as the shivering man climbed slowly with the help of the rope. Halfway up he was so tired that he almost slipped back again. But finally he managed to hook one arm over the well rim, and then it was only a question of a little more effort and he would be safe.

While Timmy and Lassie stood by and watched sympathetically, the elderly man rested a few moments, and then when he had caught his breath, climbed over the well rim and slumped to the ground. He sat with his back against the well, shaking with cold, his eyes closed. Then a giant sneeze startled both Timmy and Lassie.

"Bless you!" Timmy said politely, and Lassie said, "Wroof!"

The bearded man opened his eyes, surprised, and for the first time, a smile lighted up his face. "Why, thank you! Haven't heard that said for a long time!" Then his face went sober again, and he rubbed his hand across his forehead and muttered, "At least, not that I recollect."

"Mom says sittin' around in wet clothes is the best way to catch cold," Timmy told him solemnly. And Lassie agreed with a small bark.

The man got to his feet. "Your mom's got good sense. I better get dried off."

"I guess we'll be goin' now," Timmy said. "We're not s'posed to be here, at all. It's tres—trespassin', Dad an' Uncle Petrie said. It's breakin' the law!"

The man smiled. "Well, it's mighty lucky for me you broke the law this time!" He looked very serious and held out his hand to Timmy. "I'm much obliged, sonny. I dunno if I could've got out of there without your help."

Timmy grinned happily and took the proffered hand. But when they had shaken hands, Timmy said honestly, "It wasn't me, really. It was Lassie who heard you, an' she's the one that got the rope for you, too. So you should say thanks to her, 'stead of me."

The elderly man leaned over and held out his hand to Lassie, quite seriously. "Thank you, Lassie!"

Lassie gave him her paw and barked softly.

"She says, 'You're welcome!'" Timmy explained, beaming with pride. "Boy! Wait till I tell Mom what she did!"

The man straightened up quickly, his face suddenly darkening. "You're not to tell her! You mustn't tell *anybody* that you saw me here!"

"But why not?" Timmy was astonished and shocked.

"Because—because"—the man looked about him nervously—"because they're looking for me. They want to take me back and lock me up again!"

"Back where?" Timmy's eyes were round as saucers. "Did you run away from some place?"

"That's right, sonny. From a kind of hospital, with a big stone wall around it. They said I had to stay there, but I fooled them. I ran away when the gate was open. And nobody's going to make me go back!"

He looked so stern and angry when he said it, that Timmy felt scared for a moment. But Lassie wagged her tail and went up to the man, nudging his hand with her nose as if she were trying to tell him that she liked him. Or maybe that she felt sorry for him. Timmy decided there wasn't anything to be afraid of, when Lassie acted that way.

The stranger stroked Lassie's head, and seemed to be talking mostly to himself as he went on, "Seems like I just had to come to this place. I had to find—" He stopped abruptly and put his hand to his forehead the way he had done before. "I wish I could think of what I came here for. It was something. I keep trying to remember. But it's no use." He sighed. "I'll just keep on trying. I guess it'll come back to me soon."

"Yes, sir," Timmy agreed politely. "I sure hope so." Then he snapped his fingers to Lassie and told her, "We gotta go, Lassie. Mom said to get back early."

Lassie started off at once, eager to be on her way. Timmy had just turned to follow her, when the bearded man called to him. "Sonny! You won't tell your folks or anybody else that you found me here, will you? Promise?"

Timmy hesitated only a second. Then he said solemnly, "I promise. Cross my heart."

"Thanks, boy. I'm depending on you. Now, run along home, or your mom'll start worrying."

The elderly man in the faded cotton suit watched Timmy and Lassie trudge up the long hill. He seemed to have forgotten that he was cold and wet and that a wind was whipping through his clothing.

When the pair finally reached the top of the hill, Timmy looked back down toward the old farmhouse. The man was still standing looking up at him, and waved when he saw Timmy watching. Timmy waved back, and then climbed through the fence, with Lassie close beside him.

When they had disappeared, the man went slowly into the old barn, and the valley seemed as lonely and empty as if no one had been there for a long, long time.

The sun was almost behind the hills and the woods were full of long shadows as Timmy and Lassie hurried through on the way home. They didn't stop to look at the squirrel this time, or the birds. Timmy knew he was already late.

They passed close to the mouth of the big old cave that he and Boomer had discovered last September, but Timmy didn't even slow down. There wasn't time.

He came out about a hundred yards down the creek from the spot where he had lost his fishing pole and reel. He and Lassie had been moving so fast that he was short of breath and had to stop to catch it again. Then he saw something caught between two rocks at the edge of the water. He could hardly believe his eyes! It was his fishing pole, with the new reel still on it!

He ran down the bank to it, with Lassie close at his side. The pole was wedged in between two rocks, but it came out easily when he lifted it from above. And except that his new fishing line was hopelessly tangled around both the reel and the rod, there wasn't anything wrong with it.

But the biggest surprise was still to come! The end of his line was snagged around an old root that stuck up out of the water a few feet away, and there was a ten-inch-long speckled trout caught on his hook! The trout must have

grabbed at Timmy's bait the moment it hit the water and, in its struggles to get free, jerked the pole from his hands. The swift current had helped, too, and then had swept both the fishing pole and the trout to the bank.

Timmy grabbed up the fish, which was still wiggling. "Look, Lassie! We caught a fish! It's a lollypaloosa!" That was one of Uncle Petrie's words, and Timmy liked it because it sounded a lot bigger than ordinary words, even if he didn't know just what it meant.

Lassie took a dainty sniff at the trout, but she kept her distance from the flipping tail. Then she turned and ran up the bank toward the path. When she got to the top, she looked back down and barked sharply a couple of times at Timmy, who was still standing admiring his catch.

"Okay, I'm comin'!" Timmy called to her. "Quit scoldin'. I know it's gettin' late." He shouldered the pole, with the trout dangling from the tip of it, and climbed up to follow Lassie homeward.

Mrs. Martin was standing in the doorway, watching for him, when he came along the road with Lassie and the trout. Timmy was later than he had promised to be, but she was so relieved to see that he was safe that she let it go without a scolding.

"Look, Mom! Ain't it a whopper?" Timmy dangled the limp trout at her. "Can we have him for supper?"

"I'm afraid not, dear. Supper's all ready. But when you get your fish scaled and cleaned, we'll put it on ice for tomorrow night's supper," she smiled. "It *is* a beauty!"

"C'n I show it to Dad an' Uncle Petrie, first?"

"Of course! They're out in the barn talking to Sheriff Bennett." She was turning to go into the house, as Timmy started off toward the barn. She called after him, "I'll spread some papers on the step and you can clean your fish there."

"Thanks, Mom! I'll be right back!" he called over his shoulder, and then hurried along with Lassie close by.

He was starting into the barn, when he heard Uncle Petrie's voice, louder than usual, "I'm glad you came by to tell us, Carl. We'll be on the lookout."

"Watch yourselves, though, in case you run into the fellow," that was Mr. Bennett's voice. He was Dad's closest friend. "That traveling salesman he hitchhiked a ride with from Capitol City is pretty sure he saw the bulge of a gun in his pocket when he got out a mile north of Calverton."

"What was he in state prison for?" Dad was quite calm, from the sound of his voice.

"Armed robbery. Twenty years to life," Mr. Bennett

said. "They still don't know how he got away."

Timmy shivered. This was exciting. A real desperate criminal! And he was somewhere around Calverton!

Then he heard Uncle Petrie ask, "Got a picture of him?"

"Not yet," Mr. Bennett told him, "but we have a pretty good description of him. . . ." His voice became indistinct as the men seemed to be moving away from the door.

Timmy strained his ears, hardly daring to breathe, but he couldn't hear more than a murmur of voices now.

Lassie nudged him gently with her nose and barked softly. It was long past her suppertime, and she didn't see any use of hanging around here, dangling a dead fish.

But Timmy was thinking about what he had just heard, and slowly but surely he was coming to a frightening conclusion. Could it be—could the escaped criminal be the old man they had helped out of the well in Forbidden Valley?

Maybe he had better go right in and tell Dad all about it. He opened his mouth to call out, and then closed it again abruptly. He had given his solemn promise not to tell anybody about seeing the old man.

"Lassie," he whispered to the handsome big dog whose eyes were turned up to him with steady affection, "what shall I do?"

4
TIMMY HAS
A PROBLEM

"If I tell Dad about the man in the well, I'll be breakin' my promise," Timmy told Lassie, as he hesitated outside the barn. "And, anyhow, it couldn't be the same mean old convict they're talkin' about. *Our* old man was friendly. You liked him, so he must be all right."

That's what Timmy told Lassie—and himself. But he had misgivings. He had never kept this kind of a secret from Mom and Dad. And, after all, it *could* be the same man Sheriff Bennett was looking for!

Lassie was getting very tired of waiting around for him to come to the kitchen and give her some supper. She barked softly and took him by the sleeve, gently pulling him away from the barn and toward the house.

"All right, Lassie, I guess you're right," he told her soberly. "We better talk to Mom about it, first, and see what she thinks."

But when Timmy and Lassie reached the back step where Mom had spread out the newspaper for the fish-cleaning, he could hear her talking on the telephone.

He sat down to wait. He was beginning to feel a little dizzy, and his head felt heavy and hot. He could hardly keep his eyes open as he leaned back against the porch post and listened drowsily to Mom's voice.

Ruth Martin was trying to be polite as she listened to Miss Jenny rattling on about the escaped convict. She was trying to keep one eye on the cookstove, where two pots were bubbling merrily.

At last Ruth had a chance to cut in, "Jenny dear, thanks for calling, but I think Carl Bennett came out a few minutes ago to tell Paul about it, and *he*'ll tell me later. My potatoes are starting to stick!"

There was an excited gabble at the other end of the line, and then Ruth hung up and rushed to the rescue of the potatoes. She was just in time. They were starting to sizzle.

Timmy looked at the very dead trout that had to be

cleaned. Somehow, he didn't feel like it. "Wish you hadn't grabbed that worm," he said disgustedly. "Hey, Lassie, do you want this?" he asked hopefully. But Lassie sniffed disdainfully at it and turned away with a sharp little whine.

Ruth came out to the porch. She saw Timmy's spotted face and heavy eyes and bent over him quickly, feeling his forehead. It was burning with fever.

"Mom, there's somethin' I've got to tell you," Timmy said drowsily. "It's about the haunted house, an'—"

"Never mind it now, dear. It's too bad to spoil your birthday celebration, but you're headed for bed, right now!"

"But, Mom, it's important!"

"It can keep. Off we go, Mister Measles!" She led him inside, her arm around him to steady him.

Timmy was glad to lean against her, and to let her help him undress and get into bed. He felt awfully tired, and he wanted to sleep. But just before he drifted off, he opened his eyes and a frown puckered his forehead. "Mom, there was somethin' I wanted to ask you, but I just can't seem to remember it now."

"Don't worry, dear. It'll come back to you. Just go to sleep now."

"All right, Mom."

Ruth Martin bent and kissed the hot little forehead. "Good night, dear." But Timmy was too drowsy to do more than mumble, "Night, Mom," before he was fast asleep.

Ruth was closing the door after her when she glanced back into the room and saw that Lassie had slipped in unnoticed and was now sitting beside the foot of Timmy's bed, her chin resting on the covers.

"Come on, Lassie!" Ruth whispered. "Come get your supper!" But for once, the magic word "supper" failed. Lassie only blinked at her and didn't move. Ruth had to go in again and lead her out.

Ruth closed the door softly and patted Lassie's head. "Sorry, girl!" she whispered. "I know you hate to leave him, but he'll be all right. It's just measles, and he'll be up and around in a little while."

The house was very still at midnight. The moonlight was streaming in through Timmy's window, as he sat up in bed staring blankly about the room. "We got to find the rope," he said worriedly, "or the poor old man will drown!" He pushed back the covers and swung his feet to the floor.

A moment later, he was staggering across the room toward the door. Ruth had left it open so that she or Paul could hear if Timmy called out during the night. She had already been in twice to check on him, and found him fast asleep and still flushed with fever. Timmy moved silently on his bare feet along the hallway toward the kitchen.

But Lassie was there, on guard, lying as close to the closed kitchen door as she could get, and she heard him at once. She rose when the door started to open, and moved aside, watching curiously in the dark as Timmy groped his way dizzily toward the rear door.

When he didn't speak to her, she knew that something was the matter. She moved suddenly between him and the door. Timmy bumped into her, and tried to push her aside, muttering feverishly, "Go 'way, Lassie. I have to look for the rope!"

Lassie held her ground, though Timmy tried to walk around her to reach the door. Then she barked softly, protestingly. She couldn't seem to understand what was wrong with him.

For a moment, when Paul heard her bark, he thought she might be warning them against an intruder. The escaped convict came quickly to his mind. He leaped out of bed and ran down the hallway toward the kitchen, not even stopping to find a weapon. Ruth was right behind.

A quick glance into Timmy's empty bedroom told the story, and they hurried to the kitchen as Lassie barked again. Timmy stood blinking as the light snapped on, and they could see by the dazed look in his heavy-lidded eyes, that he had been sleepwalking in the grip of the fever.

Paul caught Timmy up in his arms. "Back to bed, young fellow!" he told him, and Timmy sighed and snuggled down with his head on Paul's shoulder.

But a few minutes later, when Paul and Ruth had him safely back in his bed and tucked in, Timmy lifted his head sleepily and peered at them. "Don't send him back, please, Dad. He's such a nice ol' man. An' Lassie likes him, too."

"Don't worry, dear. Everything will be all right!" Ruth laid a cool hand on Timmy's burning forehead. He sighed and sank back on the pillow, smiling.

They left Lassie stretched out in front of his closed door.

"What old man was he talking about? I wonder," Paul frowned. "Do you suppose there's any chance he's met—" he broke off abruptly, but a moment later he shook his head, smiling. "I guess not. If he'd met that runaway convict, he'd hardly call him a nice old man. Bennett says Sanders is a very tough character."

"He tried to tell me something about the Brunson farm," Ruth said, "but I didn't pay much attention." She looked worried. "It's farfetched, I realize, but I wonder if you ought to tell Mr. Bennett. That deserted farm *would* be a good place for someone to hide out. No one ever goes there."

"I'll think about it. I have to go into town tomorrow morning anyhow, and I may drop in to see Carl."

Dr. Wilson came by in the morning, though he didn't have to look at Timmy to know that he had caught the same fever as his pal Boomer. "Just keep him quiet for a few days," he told Ruth Martin. "And tell Lassie to stop looking so miserable. Everywhere I turn around here, I see her staring at me. She's worse than an old mother hen about that youngster!"

Paul had driven into town to get some spare parts for the plow and to look at a good secondhand tractor that he was thinking of buying. It would take most of their savings, but the tractor was badly needed, and he and Ruth had decided to do without a new stove for another year or two, to get it.

He found Carl Bennett in his office, studying the bulletin from the state prison, with Blackie Sanders' picture and record.

"Whew! He's a mean-looking character, judging by that

picture of him!" Paul commented.

"Probably flatters him, at that! Run your eye down that record."

Paul glanced at the list of Sanders' crimes. "I always suspected I didn't want to be a policeman," he said with a grim smile. "Now I'm sure of it!"

Carl Bennett sighed and dropped the bulletin into his desk drawer. "The worst part of it is not knowing where to look for him. There hasn't been even a rumor of anybody seeing him since that traveling salesman came in with *his* story. I'm hoping he kept right on hitchhiking to the ocean—*either* ocean!"

"Don't tell me you couldn't use the reward!" Paul grinned.

Carl squinted at him, and tapped the badge he wore pinned to his suspenders. "Line of duty. No reward money. But it might get me re-elected next fall—if I could find him and bring him in." Then he added, half to himself, "And didn't get shot full of holes doing it!" He chuckled, but his eyes were unsmiling.

"I might have a lead," Paul said, growing serious abruptly. And he told the sheriff about Timmy's mention of the old man and his reference to the Brunson farm.

"It probably doesn't mean a thing," Paul concluded, "but Ruth and I both thought you might like to take a look around the Brunson place, to be on the safe side."

Carl got up without answering, and went over to the map on the wall opposite his desk. With his finger, he traced the main highway from Capitol City, the road on which the salesman had picked up the hitchhiker. There were many small unimproved roads leading off from the highway as it neared the hills. As he studied the map, he nodded slowly. "The more I think of it, the likelier it gets that Sanders might be right there. I think I'll take a look this morning."

He took a service revolver from his desk drawer and checked it to see if it was loaded. Then he dropped it into his side pocket and reached for his hat. "Thanks, Paul. Even if it turns out to be a false alarm, I'm glad to be out doing something besides sitting here and waiting for word that he's used that gun on somebody."

Paul nodded understandingly. "I'd like to go along, if you say so."

"Sorry," Carl told him soberly, "I don't have an extra gun to lend you. And you can't take a chance with a killer like Sanders."

Paul smiled. "I thought of that. So I brought along my rifle. It's in the back of my car, under some sacks. I got it out of the house without Ruth seeing it."

Bennett hesitated. Then he laid his hand heavily on Paul's shoulder for a moment, and said gruffly, "All right. Come on, but don't let me catch you trying to be a hero!"

They found the gate at the end of Brunson's little valley still firmly chained shut. Grass was growing high all about the gate and as far as they could see from one end of the valley to the other. It was lush and lovely after the spring rain, but there was nowhere a sign that a human foot had touched it.

"Better leave the car here, and not break the gate lock," Bennett said. "Walking's good, and it won't give him warning that we're coming—if he's here."

"Sure looks deserted!" Paul stood off when they had come up to within a hundred yards of the house and barn.

"First time I've had a close look in years," the sheriff admitted. "The old place certainly stands up against the weather. It's been empty twenty years."

"What happened to the Brunsons?" Paul asked, as they stood under a lone maple and watched for a sign of life at either the boarded-up house or the barn.

"Brunson's wife died of an operation, suddenlike. Left a boy of ten. Brunson couldn't stand it here without her, and just picked up one day and took the boy to the city. Place has been shut up ever since."

"It's a shame," Paul shook his head. "I'd say, just at a glance, this is some of the best land in Calverton County." There was a wistful tone in Paul's voice. "Things ought to grow like wildfire here."

"Guess they did," Bennett admitted, "and it's a shame somebody can't take it over and make a good living."

"Who's handling the property?" Paul asked.

"A bank pays the taxes every year, out of a fund that Brunson left there. Some city bank on the East coast." Bennett saw the hungry look in his friend's eye, and went on, with a twinkle, "And there's no use trying to lease it. That's been tried. The bank says 'No deal.' "

"And Brunson probably living in Paris or some such place while it lies idle!" Paul scowled.

"Well, it's his, and if that's what he wants to do with it, it's his business!" Bennett grinned. "Let's move up and take a good look around. I don't think there's anybody within a mile or two, but we might as well be dead sure."

They were alert for danger as they came up to the house.

But they could see that the windows and door were heavily boarded, and there was no sign of anyone having broken in.

Carl Bennett, scanning the recently dried ground between the well and the house, stopped suddenly, pointing.

The tracks of a man's heavy shoes were all around. They had unmistakably been made since the rainstorm of night before last. They led back and forth between the barn and the half-covered well.

Carl took out his revolver, and Paul balanced his rifle, ready for a quick shot, as they followed the tracks toward the barn and around to the side door.

The small side door was open a few inches, and moving gently in the spring breeze. The two men exchanged knowing looks. The man they were hunting was either inside here, or gone.

Tense, ready, Carl Bennett motioned his friend to stand out of the line of fire, as he went up to the small door. Paul obeyed, but kept his rifle leveled toward the doorway.

Inside the old barn, high up in the darkness of the almost empty hayloft, the gray-bearded man was watching the narrow slit of light that was the doorway.

He had been waiting for this moment ever since he had seen the red-painted car stop outside the gate.

5

WHO WAS IT?

The gray-bearded man in the hayloft held his breath as he stared toward the slowly opening side door of the old barn. He lay half-hidden in the musty old hay, and wisps of it clung to his hair and beard.

The loft ladder lay beside him, and he hoped desperately that its absence would convince the men who were coming to look for him, that it had been gone as long as the barn had stood empty.

Now as he watched the door, he saw it swing wide. Then, in a flash, the square-shouldered figure of a man blotted out the sunlight. He could see that the man had a revolver in his hand.

Terrified, he looked around the loft for something he could use as a weapon. But there was nothing. Not even a chunk of wood. And it was too late for him to try to run.

The sunlight was streaming through the empty doorway again. That meant that the big man with the gun was inside.

The man in the loft shivered and put his face down in the hay. The dust from it nearly made him sneeze, but he managed to stop it in time. He could hear the men below whispering, over near the door, but he couldn't make out what they were saying.

A spot of light played on the ceiling of the hayloft and danced about searchingly for a moment. Then it was gone. It had missed the hidden man by only a few inches.

"No sign of him, now, but somebody's been here, all right." The voice had the snap of authority.

"Yes, I saw the ashes of a little fire out in back. He probably warmed up some food on it," the second man agreed. And he added, "The poor devil!"

The first man's voice had a sharp edge to it. "Save your sympathy for the people he's robbed and killed, Paul. Sanders is no better than a wild animal, judging by his list of crimes he's committed."

Their voices died away as they went to the door and out.

The gray-bearded man sat up and stared after them. "Sanders," he repeated dazedly. "My name's Sanders. And I'm a killer. I didn't know." He buried his face in his hands and sat huddled there a long time.

He didn't even lift his head to look over toward the small side door as it was slammed shut. The sound of a hammer nailing a board into place echoed through the empty barn.

After a while he lifted his head, and there was a look of bewilderment on his face. "It won't come back to me, no-how. Lord help me, I can't remember. Even the name don't seem like it belongs to me. 'Joey,' they called me at the hospital. Not 'Sanders.' Never 'Sanders' that I recollect. And if I ever killed anybody, it's gone from my mind. . . ."

Suddenly he looked frightened. "I guess maybe I better go away from here and hide someplace else. They might come back again and catch me sometime when I'm sleeping. And they'd lock me up again."

"We missed him by a couple of hours, I'd say. The ashes of his fire were still a bit warm," Carl Bennett said, as they drove back toward Calverton.

"Looks like Timmy did see him there, after all," Paul

looked serious. "If the youngster wasn't running a high fever, I'd ask him some questions. Sanders may have dropped a word about where he was going, some such thing."

"Not much chance of that. Sanders is too smart."

"Seems funny," Paul looked thoughtful, "Timmy saying he was a nice old man. And Lassie apparently taking to him, too. It certainly doesn't fit the description of Sanders that the state prison's sending out!"

Carl Bennett laughed suddenly. "Y'know, I've been thinking that myself. How do we know that was Sanders? Maybe it was some old tramp that broke into the Brunson place to get out of the rain and hung around a couple of days resting his feet."

Paul grinned back at him. "Well, we had a nice ride on a pretty spring day. So there's no harm done, either way!"

But a few days later, when Timmy's fever had finally disappeared, Ruth Martin came into the kitchen from Timmy's room with his breakfast tray, and told her husband, "Better go talk to Timmy, dear. He wants to tell you something."

Paul looked stern. "And I want to tell *him* something about breaking his promise not to go near that farm!"

Ruth smiled. "That's what is on his mind. He feels pretty bad about it. It seems some old man fell into the well there, and Lassie went to his rescue. Timmy went after her before he'd stopped to remember his promise."

"Does he suspect his 'nice old man' may have been that escaped convict, Sanders?" Paul asked grimly.

"I'm afraid he *did!*" Ruth admitted, "but I told him that Carl and you decided it was probably some harmless tramp, and he seemed a lot relieved."

"Relieved?"

"It seems he promised not to tell anyone he had seen the old man. There was something about being afraid of having to go back to some *hospital*."

"Timmy and his promises!" He shook his head and started toward the bedroom. "I'll talk to him about that."

"Paul!" Ruth looked serious, and when Paul turned with a look of inquiry, she said softly, "Don't forget he's only seven."

"Don't worry, honey!" Paul smiled. "One look from those big eyes of his, and I'll melt like a cake of ice at a Fourth of July picnic!"

Ruth laughed and blew him a kiss as he turned and went out. She knew Timmy would say he was sorry he had broken his promise, and Paul would bring in the fishing rod, with a whole spool of brand-new line to take the place of the tangled one. And they would have a grand time planning their summer fishing trip, everything else forgotten.

And that's what did happen. And Timmy was allowed up for supper, for the first time in several long days.

The next morning started an exciting day for the whole Martin household. Paul and Uncle Petrie were up at dawn getting ready to go to Calverton and pick up the newly bought tractor and drive it home.

Timmy, up and dressed as early as they were, and even more excited, hoped they would take him along. But Ruth explained gently to him that as long as he had those few little pink spots left on his face, he was better off not going into town. There wasn't any danger now of his giving the measles to other children, but not all the mothers understood that, and Ruth didn't wish to worry them.

"Mom!" Timmy had come charging in from the yard, with Lassie bounding at his heels. "What'll I do?"

"Well, there's that jigsaw puzzle Boomer's mother sent you. And you haven't looked at that book about horses that your teacher brought by."

Timmy's lower lip stuck out. Ruth could see that her suggestions weren't getting over. "Aw, I'm tired of puzzles an' picture books."

"Why don't you and Lassie go on a hike? Maybe Boomer would like to go with you. I'll fix you a nice lunch. Peanut butter and jelly sandwiches and a banana for each of you. What do you say?"

Timmy's eyes sparkled. He had a lot of things to tell his chum. "Can I call him right now?"

Ruth laughed. "I'm afraid he isn't even awake yet. The sun is barely up, you know. But I'll fix the lunch anyhow, because I'm sure he'll want to go."

Timmy's mother had guessed right. Not only did Boomer want to go on a hike, but his mother was glad to bring him over in the family car and leave him.

"It was good of you to call!" Boomer's mother looked exhausted. "He's been running us ragged. You have no idea!"

"I think I have!" Ruth laughed. "After the last couple of days!" She pointed out the kitchen window.

The boys were chasing all over the yard, shouting happily. Lassie was barking loudly as she danced around them, just as excited as they were to be out in the spring sunshine again. Now Boomer sprawled in the dust.

"And I just washed those overalls!" Boomer's mother shook her head in mock despair. "But it's wonderful to see the poor little fellows feeling so good."

Ruth agreed heartily. All the long hours of taking care of Timmy, before the fever finally broke, were forgotten now that he was well again.

The two mothers watched their sturdy youngsters start off down the road, fishing poles over their shoulders and Lassie cavorting ahead of them.

"I'm glad we don't have to worry about the Brunson farmhouse any more," Mrs. Bates said, over a cup of coffee.

"Why, what's happened there?" Ruth was surprised.

"Now, don't say Miss Jenny hasn't told you that the Brunson boy has come back and is moving into the old place!"

Ruth shook her head. "I guess she thought we were such newcomers to Calverton that we wouldn't be interested."

"Young Brunson was only a kid about Boomer and Timmy's age when his pa took him away, after the mother passed on."

"Does he have a family?"

"I don't know. All I heard is that he got the keys from

Attorney Blake last week, and said he'd move in soon.
Blake says he wasn't even too sure how to find his way to
the valley, but he said No when Blake offered to show him.
Guess he seemed like a feller with a load on his mind and
set on keeping it to himself."

"Well, as you said, we won't have to worry about the boys
climbing on that old rusty machinery any longer or falling
into the well," Ruth said thankfully.

"I hope there's a family." Mrs. Bates was already planning one of her famous angel food cakes as a welcoming
gift to the newcomers. She was a friendly person who expected everyone else to be just as friendly.

Timmy and Boomer hadn't quite made up their minds
in which direction to hike. They stopped to talk it over
before they reached the woods.

"I'll show you where I caught that whoppin' big trout,"
Timmy boasted. "Maybe I'll catch another one like it."

"Aw!" Boomer frowned. "I don't feel like fishin'. I'd
rather look at the haunted house through your spyglass."

"We'd have to go through the woods!" Timmy didn't
mind changing his plans. "We can stop at our cave an' eat
our lunch!"

"Let's climb the hill *first,* an' then come back to the cave

when the sun's shinin' toward it. It ain't so spooky in the sunshine." Boomer was an inch taller than Timmy, and it made him want to be the one who did all the planning. Which was generally all right with Timmy, who didn't care who made the plans just so he was in on them.

They left their fishing poles hidden in thick brush beside the creek, and started the long hike up the slope of Old Blue Top. Lassie ran ahead as usual.

And as they went, Timmy told Boomer all about his and Lassie's adventure with the old tramp who had fallen into Brunson's well. "But when Dad an' Mr. Bennett went out to look for him, he was gone!" Timmy concluded.

Boomer scowled. "I bet you made it all up," he said finally. "You're fibbin'."

Timmy stopped and faced him. "No! I'm not!"

"Ah, pooh!" Boomer didn't want to believe Timmy was telling the truth. Nothing so exciting had ever happened to *him*.

"I'll show you the well he fell into! Then you'll have to believe me!"

"I'm not allowed to go there! An' neither are you!"

"I mean from up on top of the hill. With the spyglass."

"Huh! A lot you could see from there!" Boomer was

beginning to be convinced. "A well's a well!"

Timmy knew he would have to add a clincher. He looked mysterious and even whispered, though there was no one within a mile but Lassie and themselves, "Mr. Bennett and Dad think maybe he was the 'scaped convict from the state prison!"

Boomer's eyes fairly popped out. "Gee!" he breathed. "The one they never did catch? The—the killer?"

Timmy could see he was almost convinced now. He nodded vigorously and added, "An' I coulda captured him if I'd had a gun!"

"Wow!" Boomer swallowed that without a bit of doubt. He stared at his pal with new respect. "Weren't you scared?"

"Uh-uh!" Timmy shook his head. "Lassie was along."

That made sense to Boomer, and they trudged on up the hill side by side, more than ever anxious to take a good look at the Brunson farmhouse. There was always a chance that the mysterious stranger would be down there again!

But when they had reached the top of the hill, and climbed to the top rail of the old fence, they didn't need the telescope to see that something new was going on down at the farmhouse.

6

THE BRUNSONS

The front door of the farmhouse was wide open now, and the heavy boards had been removed from the windows. A sedan was standing in front of the porch and a trailer piled high with furniture was hitched to it. Even from Timmy's distance on the hill, he could see that it was an old sedan, even older than his family's.

"Somebody's movin' in!" Timmy excitedly adjusted the telescope. Now he could see a little girl about his and Boomer's age, sitting in the sedan with someone who was probably her mother. A tall man in shirt sleeves was carrying a couple of cane-bottomed kitchen chairs into the house.

"There's a girl, but I don't see any guys," Timmy

frowned. He handed the telescope to Boomer with a disappointed sigh. "I guess that's all there is! A girl!"

Boomer adjusted the telescope and stared through it. "Hey!" he exclaimed, "she's gettin' out of the car, an' she's carryin' something! It looks like a—a *cat!*"

Timmy could see the white fluffy object that the little girl had set on the ground. It moved on wobbly legs. But it was certainly not a cat. It was a white puppy.

"That's a puppy!" Timmy said. "It's called a poodle. I saw one in town a long time ago!"

"It's a cat!" Boomer insisted. "I know a cat when I see it!"

As Lassie whimpered at the object below, Boomer got a bright idea. "Scat, Lassie! Go get him!"

In a flash, Lassie was bounding down the hill.

Timmy jumped up, yelling, "Lassie! Come back here!" but the big collie paid no attention to the call. "Now look what you've done!" Timmy wailed to Boomer. "She'll scare the puppy!" And then he, too, slipped through the railing and started galloping down the long hill with Boomer close on his heels, both yelling to Lassie to come back.

The woman in the car heard the yelling, and looked up. She saw a big, shaggy dog rushing down the side of the hill, followed by two boys who were yelling something.

She gave a frightened scream and jumped out of the car to run to the little girl.

"Letty!" She reached the startled little girl and caught her up in her arms, holding her tightly and staring terrified at the big collie that had almost reached the foot of the hill. "Dave! Help!" The mother was hysterical, and the little girl started to cry loudly.

The puppy had seen Lassie coming and was running to meet her now, its tiny tail wagging happily. But Dave Brunson, rushing out of the house to see what was wrong, saw only what seemed to be the attack of a vicious dog.

He looked around desperately for a weapon he could use to beat off the strange animal, but all he could find was a wooden slat that he had pulled off one of the furniture crates. With that in his hand, he ran toward the attacker.

Lassie slid to a stop. She sniffed at the small white object as it came up and in puppy fashion lay down and rolled over on its back, legs waving in the air. It was saying, as appealingly as it could, "Please don't hurt me, Big Dog. I'm just a helpless pup and I want to make friends."

Lassie's tail started swinging. But Dave Brunson didn't notice it. He saw the puppy rolling on the ground and he thought Lassie had hurt it.

Letty was screaming, "My puppy! Don't let the bad dog hurt my puppy!" and at the same time struggling to get out of her mother's arms and run to her puppy's rescue.

Timmy reached the yard a couple of seconds after Lassie and the puppy met. He saw the man running at his collie with a stick, and he ran between, yelling, "Don't hit Lassie!"

Brunson brushed him aside and kept going, but Timmy got to Lassie first, and threw himself to the ground beside her, arms around her neck. "No! Don't!" he shrieked.

But the stick was already coming down, and Brunson couldn't stop it in time. Instead of hitting Lassie, it struck Timmy a glancing blow on the shoulder, and Timmy cried out in pain.

In a flash, Lassie had leaped at Brunson and grabbed his wrist in her teeth, snarling and growling. Brunson staggered back, trying to shake her off. "Let go!" he yelled, dropping the slat.

But Lassie's teeth were clamped on the wrist of the man who had hurt her young master, and it wasn't till Timmy hollered at her to let go, that she dropped away from Brunson. She backed off, showing her teeth in a snarl and keeping between him and Timmy.

Timmy put his arm over her neck, and held her, glaring up at the man. Boomer had stayed a safe distance, and was watching, scared. "You hit me!" Timmy accused.

Dave Brunson looked worried. "I didn't mean to hit you, sonny. I was aiming at that dog of yours. I thought he was about to chew up our pup."

"Lassie isn't a he. She's a she. And she never hurt a puppy or anybody else!" He kept his arm protectingly around Lassie.

"Dave! Send them away!" Mrs. Brunson called sharply. She still clung tightly to Letty, but the little girl was struggling to get free.

"Let me down, Mamma!" she pleaded. "I want to pet the big dog!"

"No, no!" Her mother held on to her even more tightly. And then, hysterically, "Dave! Don't just stand there! Chase that awful dog away! Get him out of here!"

"We're goin' right now!" Timmy said defiantly. And as the small white puppy cavorted around Lassie, trying to tempt her to play, he said, "Go 'way, pup!" And he started toward the hill, pulling Lassie along. "Come on, Lassie!"

Boomer fell in behind, and followed across the yard.

And the puppy came right along after them.

Dave Brunson watched them start up the hill, and sighed. He was sorry he had struck the small boy, even though it had been an accident. He made up his mind he would find out who the child was, and make a point of apologizing to his parents as soon as possible. Probably someone in Calverton would know who the two boys were.

"I hope you told them never to come on our property again," Meta Brunson told her husband shakily.

"I don't think they will, dear. I think the big dog was just being friendly with Pom-Pom," he soothed her.

She had let Letty down, once the boys were out of the farmyard. Now Letty was off like a flash, after them.

"Letty!" she called. "Come back here!" But Letty was already starting up the hill after the two boys and the dogs. She plunged into the heavy brush at the base of the hill, paying no attention to the brambles that tore at her dress.

"Pom-Pom! Here, Pom-Pom!" she shouted.

Timmy and Boomer stopped and looked back, startled. They hadn't even noticed that the poodle puppy was following them and Lassie. It was only a few feet behind them, and having difficulty climbing on its very young legs.

"Shoo! Go back!" Timmy waved an arm at Pom-Pom, but the pup kept on coming. And when it reached the place where Lassie was waiting with the boys, it danced up to her and started leaping at the patient collie's ear, trying with puppy impudence to catch and worry the fascinating turned-over tip. Lassie took the assault goodnaturedly, but when the sharp little teeth nipped her ear, she growled a little and shook her head.

The puppy danced back to take another nip, and Lassie decided she had had enough. She lifted one paw and put it firmly down on the wiggling pest. The puppy yipped a protest and tried to wriggle free, but Lassie held it down in spite of its whimpering struggles. She knew she would be due for more ear-chewing the moment she let the puppy up.

Timmy and Boomer were both laughing heartily at the scene, when Letty came struggling up the hill. She misunderstood. It looked to her as if the big collie intended to make a meal of her puppy. "Pom-Pom!" she wailed, and began to cry loudly.

Lassie lifted her foot, and the puppy rolled free and bounced over to greet Letty. She was surprised and delighted, and snatched it up in her arms. Pom-Pom promptly made a frantic attempt to lick her face, its small body one big delighted wiggle.

"Lassie wasn't hurtin' the puppy," Timmy reassured Letty solemnly, and she gave him a shy smile.

But Boomer, watching the joyful reunion, snorted. "That's about the silliest pup I ever saw!" he commented. "Boy! I wouldn't ever have a pup as silly as that one!"

Letty glared at him. "He isn't silly! An' when he's grown up, he'll be the most beautiful dog in the whole world!"

"Yah!" Boomer couldn't think of any other answer.

There was a shrill call from the farmyard. "Letty! Come back here this instant!"

"Yes, Mommy!" Letty called down, and started away with the puppy in her arms. But she hadn't gone more than a couple of steps when she turned and faced the two boys, who were watching her soberly. She gave Boomer a defiant toss of her head, but she smiled sweetly at Timmy, and announced, "My name's Letty, boy. What's yours?"

Timmy looked startled. Then he said hastily, "Timmy Martin."

"Good-by, Timmy. I'll see you again!" And then she giggled, turned, and fled down the hill with Pom-Pom yapping in her arms.

"Girls!" said Boomer disgustedly. "They're all silly!"

"Lassie's a girl, an' she isn't silly!" Timmy reminded him.

"That's different," Boomer admitted seriously. "Lassie's —well—Lassie's a dog girl, an' it isn't the same as being a people girl."

Timmy wrinkled his forehead. "I guess not. Anyhow, let's have our lunch, an' then we can go to the cave."

So they trudged on up to the brow of the hill where they had left their lunch pail and the telescope, and were soon enjoying the tasty sandwiches and cookies and milk that Mom Martin had packed for them. Lassie came in for a full share of the food, as usual.

Timmy's shoulder felt sore, and he pulled off his shirt to look at the shoulder that the man had hit with the wooden slat. There was only a small bruised spot to be seen.

Boomer eyed it sympathetically. "I bet your pa'll get the police after that feller."

Timmy looked shocked. "The police?"

"Sure! They'll throw him in jail—quick! Bang!"

"But he didn't mean to hit *me!* He was after Lassie 'cause he thought she was going to bite Pom-Pom!" Timmy insisted. And he added soberly, "It wasn't his fault I got in the way."

"Just the same—" Boomer liked to argue.

Timmy interrupted, with a wide grin, "Anyhow we're even! Lassie bit his wrist. An' I bet it hurts more'n my shoulder!"

Dave Brunson's wrist did hurt. Lassie's teeth had clamped down hard when she made him drop the slat, but she hadn't broken the skin.

"That awful dog!" Meta Brunson said angrily. "If those boys and that dog ever come here again, I'm going to take a broom to all three of them!"

Her husband sighed. "That's hardly the way to get along with the neighbors. You forget we're not living in the city any longer. This is our home, and there's no sense getting off on the wrong foot with people we'll have to be friends with."

Meta frowned and looked around her at the dust that lay inch deep on everything. It would take hard work to make it into any sort of a home, she thought. And she didn't know if she wanted to make friends here.

"We should have sold this place," she said bitterly.

Dave looked at her, and his shoulders drooped dejectedly. "I tried. You know that. But the only offer we had was so low I had to turn it down."

"I still can't see why we have to *live* here!"

"Because we own it. And because it's going to do Letty a world of good to live in the country!" Dave Brunson's voice was firmer now.

"But you've never done any farming!" Meta was repeating an old argument. "You don't even know how to start!"

"There are plenty of men in Calverton who'll be glad to give me the right advice!" Dave put his arm around his wife's waist. "We'll make it somehow, honey!"

He drew her to the doorway, and they watched Letty as she and her small fluffy pup romped in the yard. She was laughing hard as the poodle tried to chase a rubber ball and tumbled all over itself.

Letty ran and caught it up in her arms, giving it an extra hard squeeze that made it yip in protest. "Oh, 'scuse me, Pom-Pom," they heard her say, "but you're such a darling!"

Then she caught sight of her parents in the doorway, and ran toward them with the pup struggling in her arms. But before she got there, the pup had freed himself and was off and running. So Letty had to chase him again. "Come back here, you naughty puppy!" she called.

Meta Brunson's face softened as she and Dave laughed

at their daughter. She rested her cheek against her husband's shoulder. "Maybe it *will* work out. I'll try to do all I can to help."

Dave smiled at her. "I know you will, dear. And it's bound to be great here for Letty. Why, I remember Dad saying how sickly I was when they brought me here when I was a baby. And when he and I left, I was as strong as an ox. The valley did it!"

Meta smiled faintly. "I don't want a lady ox for a daughter, Dave Brunson. I'll settle for a healthy little girl, if you don't mind!"

Letty had given up chasing the puppy by now, and came running up, a little out of breath. "His name's Timmy Martin," she announced.

"Whose name, baby?" Meta smiled, brushing the hair out of Letty's eyes.

"Why, the boy that owns that lovely big dog! Can he come back again soon an' play with Pom-Pom an' me?"

"We'll see what can be done about it, honey," Dave assured her quickly. But when he glanced at Meta, he saw that she was frowning, and her lips were set.

"You'd better help me get the stove set up," she told Dave, "or we won't have any supper tonight!"

7
THE CAVE

When Timmy and Boomer came down off the hill and started home through the woods, the sun was still high overhead. They stopped beside the creek where their fishing poles were hidden under the bushes.

"Let's fish awhile," Boomer suggested. "We got lots of time."

"You can fish if you want to," Timmy told him, "but I want to see if anybody's been in our cave an' took my rock collection while we've been havin' the measles."

"Guess I'll go, too," Boomer agreed. His legs were aching from all the climbing uphill and downhill, but he couldn't let Timmy think he was tired.

So they set out, following a trail by means of certain mysterious markings they had carved on small tree trunks along the way, in approved Indian scout style. Not that they needed anything to guide them, after several visits, but trailing was more fun than just going straight to the cave.

Their special cave was in a part of the "unimproved" woods section of the countryside. Because of some rocky hills that rose up abruptly in the path of the original wagon road, the first settlers had detoured around the section.

Since that time, several generations of small Calverton boys had discovered the cave and claimed it as their own, a hideaway far from the everyday world. And growing up, they had been sentimental about it, and had left it very much as they had found it—a relic of the days when hardy pioneers had taken shelter there from Indian raiders.

In the past thirty or forty years, with the coming of automobiles and paved roads, and a bicycle for practically every boy from the age of six upward, Calverton folks had just about forgotten "the old Injun cave" that their grandfathers had known. The only way to it was to struggle through tangled underbrush, scramble over rocks, and wade a couple of small brooks. Which of course made it a very special secret to the discoverers.

They were trudging along now, pushing through tall brush that seemed to have grown enormously in all directions since their last visit before the big storm. Lassie was as usual, trotting ahead, alert for danger, stopping every now and then to sniff the air and look about her sharply.

The tall trees, with their masses of new leaves, met and interlaced overhead, making a sort of green umbrella that almost shut out the warm spring sun. The few shafts of sunlight that filtered down through the leaves were tinged with a pale green. The woods seemed filled with the color.

Boomer looked at Timmy and laughed. "You oughta see your face! It's green!"

"Huh!" Timmy grinned back, "no greener'n yours, I bet!" Then Timmy stopped grinning. He saw that Lassie had come to a sudden halt up ahead, and was growling at something in the bushes. Now she backed toward him and Boomer, inch by inch, never taking her eyes off whatever it was that she had discovered.

"Wh-what is it, Lassie?" Timmy whispered, and clutched Boomer's sleeve. They stood close together, trying to peer past Lassie and see what had upset her.

"C'n you see anything?" Boomer's voice quavered.

"Uh-uh," Timmy shook his head and swallowed hard.

"Maybe it's a bear!" Dad had told him there hadn't been a bear in those woods for fifty years, but he was quite sure that nothing smaller than a grizzly would have made Lassie act so scared!

Boomer pulled his sleeve free. "I'm goin' home!" he announced loudly, and a second later he was crashing away through the bushes back toward the creek.

"Come back, Lassie!" Timmy was tempted to run after Boomer, but he couldn't desert Lassie.

She had stopped backing toward him now, and was standing, head lowered, watching something Timmy still couldn't see. "Lassie! Come on!" he called. And then, when Lassie still didn't move, he ran toward her intending to grab her by the collar and drag her back from whatever the danger might be.

But when he reached Lassie and looked where her nose was pointing, his own eyes got big and round with surprise.

Not ten feet ahead, squarely in the path they had to take to the cave, were four baby skunks. They were playing like kittens, tumbling and wrestling and nipping at each other.

And just as Timmy saw them, the mother skunk ran in and got between her babies and the boy and dog. Her bright little eyes glared at the intruders, and then she started moving slowly and deliberately toward them.

"Quick, Lassie! 'Fore she turns around an' lets go!" Timmy turned and ran, with Lassie bounding along at his heels.

Mother Skunk stopped and sat down to watch them disappear into the woods. Then, with an air of having accomplished what she had set out to do, she went back to her family, herded them together with a few gentle nudges, and led them off. She didn't hurry in the least. She seemed to feel certain that the enemy wouldn't return.

Timmy and Lassie caught up with Boomer before they had gone very far, and Timmy told what Lassie had seen in their path. "Golly, am I glad she stopped us in time!"

Boomer nodded wisely. "Pa says the only way to argue with a skunk is to stay off a good twenty feet and holler. An' even then, if the wind's right, you still might have to bury your clothes till the smell's off 'em!"

They agreed it would be foolish to try to get to the cave that day. There was always a chance that Mother Skunk and her brood were still in the way.

So they headed for home. The cave would be there another day. They had plenty of time. There wasn't much chance of anybody else finding it, with the brush so high.

But somebody *had* found it! At that very moment, a little wisp of smoke was curling out of the mouth of the cave and losing itself in the clear air. And if anyone had been close enough to get a whiff of that smoke, they would have smelled the aroma of broiling fish!

Deep in the old hiding place, the gray-haired man who called himself Joey was leaning over a small wood fire and watching a small trout sizzling on the end of a green twig. It was a primitive way to cook, but it was better than eating raw fish.

Joey had broken out of the Brunson barn five days ago, as soon as Carl Bennett and Paul had driven away in the red car. He had retrieved his small food supply and water can from where he had hidden them in the old hayloft when he had seen the two men drive up to the farm gate.

Then he had climbed to the top of Old Blue and plunged down its other slope into the woods. And for two days, he had hidden there, without seeing anyone, but always fearful that the law would catch up with him.

Finally, his food used up, Joey had made a twilight visit to Calverton. He had slipped into a small grocery on the far edge of town to spend his last dollar for lard, beans, and flour. He had waited till the grocer was alone.

Sam Moss had spent twenty-five years behind the counter of his small grocery and notions store. He had waited on the tall, bearded man with hardly a second look. He had been anxious to close up and get home so that he could take his shoes off, and hoboes of all kinds were no novelty in Calverton. They drifted through every springtime, as soon as the weather turned warm. And he saw nothing about this old fellow that looked different from his fellow tramps.

So Joey had disappeared back into the woods with his small stock of food. It was only after Sam had gotten comfortable in his old easy chair on the home porch, that he had wondered if he hadn't heard something last week about Sheriff Bennett looking for a bearded escaped convict.

"Shucks!" He settled down with his paper. "No chance of this feller being him. He had a sad look, but he certainly didn't look like a killer!"

The next morning Joey had stumbled onto the secret cave as he pushed deeper into the woods.

The cave made an ideal place to hide, warm and dry. There was even a small cotton blanket which someone had left there not too long ago, and a pile of firewood. The blanket kept off the night cold, and by day he used the old dusty firewood for his cooking. From somewhere deep in his memory, he recognized that he was lucky to have found the old wood. It would burn with much less smoke than newly gathered kindling, and that was important to a man who was in hiding. The less smoke, the smaller chance that anyone would see it and find him.

He had made several friends during his short stay. A doe and her fawn had come sniffing around the mouth of the cave. He had gathered a handful of tender green grass and coaxed them closer. When they had shown no great fear of him, he thankfully decided that few hunters came to this part of the woods.

Now the fawn and its mother came early each morning, the first of a string of visitors. There was a family of wood-chucks who lived in holes nearby, and popped out to stare at him, wiggling their tiny ears. They accepted the cold biscuit crumbs he threw to them, but ducked out of sight when the noisy squirrel came leaping through the branches overhead to demand his share of the spoils.

Joey fed him, too, chuckling over his boldness.

A great many birds came there, too. Some sang and then flew away. Others, like the bluejay with its raucous squawk, swooped down to chase the little ones away from the scattered crumbs.

Joey tried to see that they all had something to eat, but his supply of flour was beginning to get low. And he had no money to buy more. "We got to go slow, boys," he told the woodchuck family, but he wasn't too much worried. He was beginning to feel almost safe here.

It was only now and then that he had bad moments, thinking back to the things the man with the badge had said about him. Then he would try desperately to bring back the memory of his past, but he never could.

That night, Timmy was quieter than his parents were used to. Usually, he bubbled over with stories about things he had seen and done on his hike. Instead, he didn't seem to want to talk about it at all. He just picked at his supper and pushed his dessert away untouched.

Ruth and Paul exchanged worried looks. Then Paul asked lightly, "What's on your mind, skipper?"

"Nothin' much!" Timmy squirmed uneasily.

Ruth leaned over and felt his forehead. "I shouldn't have let you and Boomer take that long hike today. It was too soon."

"Do I have the measles back?" Timmy seemed to brighten at the thought.

"No, dear," Ruth smiled, "you're all over them. But you're going straight to bed after supper, and no radio programs for you tonight."

Uncle Petrie looked over at Timmy's sober face and gave an amused snort. "I do believe he misses all the babying!" He was only teasing, to make Timmy smile, but it didn't work. Timmy just sat looking down at the table.

Paul laughed. "Not Timmy! He's not a baby, are you, son?"

Timmy looked at him without a smile and sighed. "No, sir."

"Well, then, man to man, what's bothering you?" Paul looked serious now.

Timmy sighed again. "I guess I better tell you, only Boomer said—" he broke off, wrinkling his forehead in a worried frown.

"What did Boomer say, dear?" Ruth asked gently.

"He said you'd get the police after the man. An' it wasn't really his fault, honest! He didn't mean to hit me!" Timmy poured it out without taking a breath.

"Timmy! Who hit you? What's all this about?" Paul demanded sternly.

Timmy gulped and hesitated. Ruth laid her hand quickly

over his on the table. "Go on, dear. We'll understand."

"Out with it!" Paul frowned. This might be serious.

"Well—it's about me an' Lassie. We tres-"—he had a little difficulty with the word—"we trespassed. An' the man thought—" A knock at the door interrupted him.

They all looked startled, and then Uncle Petrie got up and hurried over to open it.

A stranger stood in the doorway. At least, he was a stranger to the three older people. But Timmy knew him. It was the man from the haunted house. The very one he had just been starting to tell them about!

He had a coat on now, and his hair was neatly combed, but there was no mistaking he was the same man. Lassie recognized him, too, and she got up from where she had been lying beside Timmy's chair, and started stalking toward the door, her head lowered, and a deep growl in her throat.

Uncle Petrie caught her by the collar and held her back. "Whoa, there, girl! That's no way to say hello!"

"I'm afraid I don't blame her!" The stranger smiled faintly. "I'm David Brunson." He seemed to think that would explain Lassie's growl.

Uncle Petrie and the Martins looked puzzled, but Paul

rose and went to the door with his hand outstretched. "Glad to know you. We heard that you and your family were moving back into the old family place."

Dave Brunson took Paul's hand in a hearty handshake, but now it was his turn to look puzzled. "Didn't the youngster tell you what happened there today?"

Paul looked startled. "At your place? Why, no!"

Timmy's voice interrupted. It was a very small voice. "I was just beginnin' to."

Paul frowned. What was it Timmy had started to tell them about a man striking him?

Dave Brunson saw the frown. "The whole thing was a misunderstanding. I thought the dog was vicious, and I was trying to drive it off."

Ruth had come over to them. "I believe that's what Timmy was telling us when you knocked. Why don't you come in and have a cup of coffee with us, and we'll find out what our son was doing on your property, after promising to keep off it?"

8

GETTING ACQUAINTED

"I'm glad you came by." Paul Martin was walking to the Brunson car with Dave.

Dave had told the Martins what had happened that afternoon, and had been relieved to find that they realized that he hadn't meant to strike Timmy. Timmy had promised that he and Lassie wouldn't "trespass" again. He would wait to be invited.

"We'll be settled in a few days, and then we'd like you folks to come and have coffee with *us,*" Dave had told Ruth as he left.

"Indeed, we'll be glad to come!" Ruth had assured him.

But now, as he and Paul crossed the farmyard to the old

car, Dave Brunson spoke frankly.

"My wife has lived in the city all of her life. It may take her a while to get used to country life, especially the—" he hesitated, hoping Paul wouldn't take offense, "the social life. I remember, when we lived here, Mother always had the house full of Ladies' Aiders and her Sewing Circle. But Meta's never had time to make many friends, with our delicate little girl on her hands."

"I'll tell Ruth to slip a little hint to the Calverton ladies to take it slow. But I think Mrs. Brunson will like them when she gets to know them."

"I think so, myself," Dave smiled. "I know Mother managed to be happy, even though there wasn't much money around. What Dad couldn't afford, we did without. And never missed it, while Dad and I had her." He looked sad, suddenly, remembering.

"She passed away before you left Calverton, didn't she?" Paul didn't intend to pry, but he sensed that Dave Brunson wanted to talk.

Dave nodded. "That's why we went. Dad couldn't stand the place without her. It was like—like he was only half alive after she'd gone. He boarded up the place and we went to live in the city."

"You must have missed the valley," Paul said quietly.

"I did, for awhile. But I was only ten, and life in the city was pretty exciting for a kid. That is, till Dad went into the army after Pearl Harbor, and didn't come back." He gave a twisted grin. "I bounced around for quite a few years, but I never thought much about the old house until the doctors told us Letty needed to get out of the city. Then we—" he hesitated a moment, and then corrected himself, "*I* decided to try to make a go of the farm, and see at the same time if it would help Letty get strong."

Paul laughed. "It will! All you have to do is look at Timmy and our little neighbor, Boomer, for proof of what fresh milk and home-grown vegetables can do!"

"I hope you're right!" Dave sighed. "I'm gambling all I've got on it!"

Paul Martin watched his visitor's old sedan disappear down the road into the darkness, coughing and rattling in the rutted dirt. As he turned to go back into the house, he was thinking, "From the looks of that old car, they haven't much to gamble with!"

Later, he talked it over with Ruth, and she agreed that it would be better to let the Brunsons get settled before anyone went calling. She meant to be quite firm about it with

Boomer's mother, Mrs. Bates, who was already making plans to drop in and welcome the newcomers right away.

It was only a few days later that Timmy came dashing into the Martin kitchen, where his mother was ironing. "Mom! Mom! I just saw Mr. Brunson! An' he says he's bought a pony for Letty!" The screen door slammed as Lassie followed him in.

"A pony!" Ruth felt a little twinge. That was one of the things she and Paul had talked about getting for Timmy this spring, but they had had to postpone it because of the new tractor. "Why, that's fine!"

"He says Letty's going to learn to ride! An' I can come see the pony!" He was breathless with excitement. "Can we go today? Me an' Lassie?"

"It seems a little soon, dear! Better wait till Letty's had a chance to get acquainted with the pony herself."

Timmy looked disappointed for a moment. Then he brightened again. "Well, can I go tell Boomer about it?"

"Of course! But be back early!"

"Yes, Mom!" And a moment later, the door slammed after him and Lassie.

Timmy found his pal Boomer out in the Bates barn, busily hammering together a somewhat rickety chicken coop for the baby chickens his folks had promised him. He didn't seem very excited about Letty's pony. In fact, he sniffed at the idea.

"Ponies are too much trouble," he said flatly. "I wouldn't have one. They gotta be brushed an' fed, an' things like that, all the time."

"I guess I wouldn't mind," Timmy sighed wistfully. "It might be fun."

"Not me!" Boomer hammered vigorously at a crooked nail.

"What's that for?" Timmy pointed to the half-finished coop.

"My chickens, when I get them," Boomer informed him. "I'm gonna keep 'em in here till they get big. Then I'm gonna sell them an' buy a new bicycle!"

"How many you gettin'?" Timmy was just as impressed as Boomer hoped he would be.

"Oh, maybe a hundred or so!" Boomer boasted.

Timmy eyed the small lopsided structure doubtfully. "They're sure gonna be crowded!"

"Oh, I'll make it bigger," Boomer assured him, "in plenty of time." But he looked at it with a growing doubt, now that Timmy had planted the seed in his mind. And a moment later he dropped the hammer. "It's too hot to hammer. Let's go wadin'."

Lassie barked and sat up, waving her paws at Timmy.

"Hey! She wants us to go!" Timmy interpreted. And Lassie started leaping around as if she understood what they were saying.

"Okay," Boomer agreed. "But we better take some sandwiches. I'll tell Mom."

But Mrs. Bates had driven into Calverton to attend a meeting of the Sewing Sisters of her church, so the boys had to make their own sandwiches. And the sandwiches that they made and wrapped in yesterday's newspaper were somewhat different from Mrs. Bates's usual peanut butter and jelly concoctions. They were skyscrapers!

By the time Boomer had put together a slice of last night's roast beef, some cold bacon, some jelly, and an inch thick gob of peanut butter topped with pickle slices, the top piece of bread was three inches from the bottom one!

And Timmy had to have the same mixture in his sandwich.

So they were well equipped for their expedition as they set out with Lassie for the woods.

But when they got to the edge of the creek and Boomer

stuck a timid toe into the water, it was a lot colder than they had expected. He said, "Ow!" and pulled his toe out in a hurry. "It's too cold!"

Even Lassie, after daintily taking a drink at the water's edge, backed away and shook herself. Timmy could see that she agreed with Boomer!

"What'll we do instead?" he asked. "I'm not hungry yet."

"Let's go to the cave!" Boomer suggested. "It's cooler. An' we can be hunters hidin' from Indians."

"Swell!" Timmy agreed.

So Boomer put on his shoes again and they set out through the woods. Lassie trotted ahead, keeping a sharp eye out for another skunk family, while the boys made believe that there were hostile Indians tracking them to get their scalps.

But the only thing that got in their way today was the thick brush and its thorns that snatched at their clothes. And in a little while they had pushed through the worst of it and were almost in sight of the cave.

Lassie ran ahead and went out of sight.

"She knows where we're going!" Timmy grinned, and began to hurry.

But when they came up to the big clump of rocks that were their final landmark, they heard Lassie barking excitedly.

"Skunk!" Boomer stopped in his tracks.

But Timmy, knowing Lassie's barks, shook his head. "It sounds more like she's glad to see somebody. That's her 'Hello' bark!"

"Maybe somebody's found our cave!" Boomer scowled.

"An' my rock collection!" Timmy looked worried.

Boomer wasted no time. "Come on! We'll just tell whoever it is that we found the cave first, an' they got to go!"

They hurried on, spurred by Lassie's strangely friendly barks. It was most likely some of the kids from the Calverton school. They both hoped they weren't big ones!

When they came in sight of the cave, all they could see at first was Lassie's rear end as she faced somebody inside. It looked as if it had turned out to be an old friend, because Lassie's tail was waving a mile a minute. But for a moment, because of the darkness of the cave, they couldn't make out who the friend was.

"Lassie!" Timmy's voice was a little sharp. There was a teeny bit of jealousy in it.

Then a man stepped out into the sunlight, and Timmy

recognized him. "Hi!" he greeted the gray-bearded man. And he told Boomer excitedly, "It's him! The man who fell in the well at the Brunson farm!" And he ran forward, with Boomer close on his heels, to shake hands.

Joey was glad to see Timmy again, and his eyes brightened at sight of what Timmy called "only our lunch" in the newspaper-wrapped packages. He was sick and tired of fish, and getting so low on beans and flour that he had to dole both out sparingly. Even his friendly little animal pets had been on short rations the last couple of days.

Timmy was happy about being able to show the man to Boomer, because Boomer never had believed Timmy and Lassie had really helped anybody out of the Brunson well. Now Timmy had the living proof of it.

"That's right!" the gray-haired man told Boomer. "I'd a'been down there yet, if Timmy hadn't come along with this smart dog of his!"

That having been settled, Boomer discovered he was getting hungry. So he sat down and unwrapped his sandwich, and began to eat it without noticing the old man's hungry looks.

But Timmy had gone inside the cave to check on his rock collection, and he had noticed the almost empty flour sack and the scant half cup of beans on the wooden shelf. And when he came out again, he saw Joey's eyes.

Timmy unwrapped his own sandwich, and then pushed it aside. "I guess I don't feel hungry," he told Boomer. "An' you always cut the bread too thick."

"It's how I like it!" Boomer mumbled through an over-stuffed mouth. "Give it to Lassie if you don't want it!"

"She doesn't like pickles, an' peanut butter sticks to her teeth," Timmy explained. Then he shook his head sadly, "But it sure is a shame it has to go to waste!"

"If you're real sure you don't want it . . ." Joey's voice trailed off.

"Golly, would you eat it for me?" Timmy made believe he hadn't even thought of that before. "Mom says it's wrong to throw away good food, so if you'd eat it for me, I'd be much obliged!"

"Thanks, sonny. Guess I can manage it!" Joey took the sandwich slowly, and even held back from biting into it right away. But Timmy could see by the size of the bite he took when he did start to eat, that he was good and hungry.

Boomer had eaten half his sandwich when he decided he'd had plenty. He lifted his arm to toss the remains into the bushes, but Timmy stopped him by calling out, "Don't be a litterbug! Don't be a litterbug!" in the singsong of the first grader.

Boomer stopped midway in his throw. "I wasn't going to do it," he scowled. "I was just pretendin'."

Old Joey suddenly said, "Sh-h-h!" and put a finger to his lips. They both looked startled and a bit scared. Joey's eyes twinkled, and he pointed over at the brambly thicket. "Look there!" he whispered.

They both stared, but for a moment they couldn't see anything in the bushes. At Timmy's elbow, Lassie lifted her head and stared, too. But she didn't growl, and the tip of her tail wagged gently.

Now they could see something moving, and make out the outlines of two deer, a doe and her fawn. Then two brown heads were thrust through the bushes, to stare back at the group out of great soft brown eyes.

"Watch, and hold real still!" Joey whispered. Then he slowly tossed a piece of Boomer's bread to the deer. It fell on the ground in front of the doe.

For a moment the doe ignored the bread, staring suspiciously at the two boys and the dog. Then, swiftly, she pushed out of the bushes, snatched up the bread in her

teeth, and in a moment had backed out of sight again. A second later, the fawn's head disappeared, too, and then the boys heard them both crashing off through the brush and scampering away.

Both boys were delighted. "Will they be back?" Timmy asked excitedly.

"Throw some more bread and they'll come back!" Boomer ordered, but Joey looked over at Lassie, who was sitting up straight now, staring after the deer and making little worried noises in her throat. "I doubt it, son. I'm afraid they won't come around again while Lassie's here. They don't know she wouldn't hurt them." He picked up the remainder of Boomer's sandwich, and wrapped it in the newspaper again. "I'll save the rest of this bread for them to eat tomorrow."

"Let's go home," Boomer suggested. Now that the show seemed to be over, and he had had enough to eat, he was getting bored with Timmy's friend.

"Okay," Timmy agreed, and scrambled to his feet. "They were cute. I hope we can see them again."

"I've got some other folks around here maybe you'd like to get acquainted with, too. Some of them are so friendly, they'll come right up and eat out of your hand!" Joey smiled at his two young visitors.

"We'll sure be back!" Timmy assured him. "Real soon!"

"Meantime," the gray-haired man said soberly, "I'd take it as a favor if you boys wouldn't tell anybody you saw me here."

Boomer frowned. "How long you gonna use our cave?"

"Just a few days, son," Joey assured him, "then I'll be drifting on. I'm just resting here."

"I guess it's okay, then," Boomer conceded, ignoring Timmy's frown, "if we get it back soon."

"You can stay as long as you like!" Timmy told the gray-bearded man firmly. And then with a defiant look at his pal Boomer, "An' we won't say anything about it because me an' Boomer have got a solemn pledge not to tell *any*body *any*thing that happens in our cave." He waited for Boomer to admit it, but Boomer just looked sulky and kicked at the ground. Timmy persisted, "Haven't we?"

Boomer squirmed and scowled, but he finally got out a "Yeah." But he still wasn't too happy about somebody else enjoying their special cave. He glanced up at the sun and told Timmy abruptly, "We gotta hurry. It's gettin' late." He started to turn away, then remembered his manners. "Good-by, Mister—say, what's your *name?*"

"Joey," the old man said softly. "That's it. Joey."

"Just Joey?" Boomer looked startled. "What's your other name, the one people write on your letters?"

"Got no other one. Don't really need it, seeing I don't get any letters," Joey told him soberly. "Joey's enough."

Boomer eyed him sharply. It didn't sound right to him.

"Aw! C'mon! You were in such a hurry! Let's go!" Timmy couldn't see the point of wanting to know Joey's last name. "Joey" was a nice easy name to remember.

So Boomer and Timmy started off for home, with Lassie trotting ahead.

Joey watched them go out of sight among the trees, and shook his head grimly. "I sure wouldn't want those nice little fellers to know I'm hiding from the law!"

9

THE HELPING HAND

They were hardly out of sight of the cave before Boomer said, "Let's hurry! We got to tell Mr. Bennett where he's hiding!"

"But we can't! We promised!" Timmy was shocked.

"But you said your pa thought he was the 'scaped convict! Maybe we can get a reward for capturing!" Boomer reminded him.

Timmy held back. His face was a little red as he confessed. "I guess I fibbed. He *isn't* the convict. I know."

"Yah!" Boomer scowled at him. "*How* do you know?" He looked suspicious. "You're just making it up."

"If I tell you, will you promise not to tell anybody, cross

121

your heart?" Timmy whispered mysteriously, though the only possible hearer was Lassie, waiting impatiently for them to start walking again.

"Uh-huh!" Boomer agreed, hastily making the required gesture. "Go ahead."

So Timmy told him about the old man having run away from some hospital. "An' he has to hide, or they'll drag him back an' lock him up. An' he hates it."

"Is that all?" Boomer was disappointed. He had expected something a lot more exciting, maybe spies and stolen maps, like the picture stories in the comic books.

"That's plenty!" Timmy assured him stoutly. "I guess he had to take shots, an' stay in his room. I guess you'd run away, too."

"Yeah," Boomer nodded thoughtfully. "Maybe it *would* be mean to let them find him."

So they trudged on home, chattering and trying to guess what kind of wild animals old Joey would have to show them when they went back to the cave next time. Timmy rather hoped for a bear, while Boomer favored a mountain lion.

But old Joey wasn't thinking of his wild pets just then. He was still very hungry, as he took the newspaper wrappings off the sandwich Timmy had given him. There was a lot of the thick sandwich left, enough for two or three good bites now, and plenty for the morning.

Then, as he started to eat, his eyes wandered to the headlines in the paper he had tossed aside. All of a sudden his appetite was gone.

He stared at the words that seemed to jump out at him. CONVICT STILL AT LARGE the top line in the *Calverton Tribune* read, and below it, SEARCH GOES ON IN WIDE AREA FOR DESPERATE CRIMINAL.

He put aside the sandwich and picked up the paper with a hand that shook. "No trace of the dangerous Blackie Sanders has been found since he was reported in the vicinity of our town nearly two weeks ago," he read. "Sheriff Bennett promises to keep a sharp lookout for the escaped convict, though he is of the opinion that the man Sanders has escaped into one of our neighboring states by this time and is in hiding there."

Joey sighed with relief as he laid the paper down. He was safe so long as he could stay hidden.

He didn't think the boys would tell about seeing him. But if it did slip out, and a search party came, Joey felt that he was familiar enough with the woods now, to slip away

from the cave in time and hide in one of the many thickly
overgrown hollows he had discovered.

Timmy woke up even before Lassie had made her cus-
tomary visit to his bedroom to pull off his covers and roust
him out of bed. He sat up in bed and tried to think what
it was he wanted to do today. Something had made him
wake up early, but what?

Then he remembered. He and Boomer were going out to
the cave to see old Joey. This time, he was going to ask
Mom for some apple pie. He was sure Joey would like
Mom's apple pie. And he would take along some of last
night's biscuits, if there were any left. The birds and the
squirrels would like them.

But as he sat up in bed, planning, he suddenly realized
that there was no sunshine pouring in through the window.
Either it was awfully early, or—he hated to think it could
happen—it was raining again!

His second guess was right. It was raining. Not a brisk
little shower, the kind that everybody liked to see in spring
because it freshened up the new green leaves and perked
up the flowers. Not the kind where it would be raining one
minute and sunning the next. No, this was one of those

light, steady rains. The kind that kept on, and on, till everything was muddy. Sometimes it lasted for days, first a soft, quiet rain like this one, and then a hard downpour that raised the creek till it flowed over its banks.

There was no telling how long it would keep up now. One thing was certain, though. He and Boomer wouldn't get back to the cave today. Or maybe not for a couple of days.

He flopped back on his pillow and pulled up the covers. No use now getting up early. He would sleep till Lassie came in and dug him out.

Ruth Martin was being quieter than usual as she moved around the kitchen, getting breakfast for Paul and Uncle Petrie, who were out in the barn doing the chores.

Lassie was lying close to the hall door, with her head between her paws. She was pretending that she was dozing, waiting for word to go wake up Timmy, but when Ruth pulled out the chairs at the table and spread the checkered cloth, Lassie lifted up her head and looked eagerly for Ruth to say, "Go wake Timmy!"

"Not yet," Ruth told her softly. "We'll let him sleep awhile this morning."

Lassie gave a long sigh and settled down again.

"Sometimes," Ruth told the intelligent big collie, "I think you can understand just about everything we say."

"And some of the things that we just *think!*" Paul chuckled. He had pulled off his muddy boots on the back steps, and was in his socks, carrying his dripping raincoat and hat. "I hope she doesn't read my mind right now! I'm thinking some mean things about this weather coming right when I had the south field ready to sow!"

"Think how much worse off you'd be if you hadn't had the weather bureau's radio warning that the storm was on its way! You'd have planted that field yesterday!" Ruth laughed.

"And it would have been washed out by now!" Paul agreed. "Glad I wasn't farming forty years ago! I wonder why they didn't all go bankrupt!"

Uncle Petrie was coming in as Paul spoke. He hung up his wet slicker and hat, and padded over to the sink to wash up beside his nephew. "They tell me the old-timers counted on their rheumatics to warn them about sloppy weather. Some folks still claim it works."

"I'll depend on the bureau!" Paul grinned. "That's one service we farmers would be glad to pay for!"

"That reminds me," Ruth brought the coffee over as the

men finished washing up and sat down in their places, "Miss Jenny says the Brunsons haven't ordered a phone yet."

"Can't figure anybody not wanting a phone. 'Specially with a sick young'un in the house," Uncle Petrie frowned.

Paul looked thoughtful. "Might be the expense. Stringing a wire out to their valley would cost them considerable."

"It'd be worth it. Then Brunson could get the weather by phone, till the electric company got around to running a power line to his place," Uncle Petrie insisted.

"I've got a feeling the Brunsons aren't too well fixed," Paul said, frowning.

"What makes you think that?" Ruth was surprised.

"That ancient car he drives. And I hear he's using that old plow of his father's that's been standing out in the open for twenty years. And hiring a horse to pull it!"

"No tractor?" Ruth was shocked.

Uncle Petrie and Paul both laughed at her expression.

"There's a lot of places left in the world where they haven't heard of tractors!" Uncle Petrie grinned at her.

"But everyone in Calverton uses them. And I think it's a shame if the Brunsons can't afford one, and nobody offers to lend them one!" Ruth flashed at the two men.

Paul and Uncle Petrie stopped grinning suddenly, and Paul told her soberly, "You're right as usual, Ruth. And as soon as the rain stops, I'm going to take a ride over to Brunson's and see how they're making out."

"We won't be needin' the tractor, after we get the south field seeded. Maybe you could lend it to them," Uncle Petrie suggested.

"I had that in mind," Paul agreed.

A sudden heavy downpour almost drowned out his words, and they all looked apprehensively toward the windows. The rain was coming down in such sheets that they couldn't even see the side of the barn.

"Wow! A lot of planting's gonna be washed out today!" Uncle Petrie predicted.

Dave Brunson stood on the edge of the field that he had plowed and seeded just yesterday, with back-breaking labor. It was a sea of mud in all directions. The carefully mounded earth around the seeds of his hybrid corn had been flattened out by the downpour. Even the furrows had been almost destroyed by the crosscurrent that had swept down off the hill at the height of the storm.

He had all his labors to do over again.

It was a dismal prospect. But worst of all was the thought of having to tell Meta of the disaster. They had counted on the cornfield. Their crop was to pay for some of the comforts they had to do without now—a stove that wasn't falling apart, a new pump in the kitchen sink.

Instead, he would have to get more seed, rent the plow horse again, and go through all the hard work once more. Maybe only to see another storm wash away the new planting!

He started back along the muddy road toward the farmhouse, and hardly heard the car that had come up behind him. A voice called out, "Brunson!" and he turned, startled.

It was Paul Martin at the wheel, and his wife and Timmy were in the rear seat with Lassie between them.

"Hope you don't mind people dropping in!" Paul called. "I wanted to talk to you, and the whole family wished themselves along!"

"Why—" Dave's hesitation was very slight. He wasn't sure how Meta would take the unexpected visit. She wasn't used to the easy informality of the country. "Why, of course! My wife will be happy to see you folks. I've been telling her what pleasant neighbors we have."

Timmy leaned forward hastily. "Lassie won't scare the

puppy. I warned her to be real gentle."

"I'm sure you did! And I don't think the puppy will be the least bit afraid!" Dave laughed. "Might be the other way around. Pom-Pom's teeth get sharper every day!"

He climbed into the front seat of the sedan, and rode with them into the yard.

Meta Brunson glanced out of the window and saw the car pull in. She drew back in dismay. For a moment she thought of running to the bedroom and locking herself in. She hated to meet strangers in an old faded house dress.

The kitchen was clean. Even the old stove was polished and shining. But everything in the room seemed to have poverty written all over it.

She whipped off her apron, smoothed her hair, and ran to the living room. The few sticks of furniture seemed lost in the big old room, but there was a cheerful fire on the hearth, and the curtains she had just hung up today—made of old sheets and dyed a pretty pale pink—were fresh and perky.

She could hear the voices of her visitors as they came toward the porch, and she steeled herself to smile her warmest when she greeted them. She opened the door, smiling.

But when she saw Timmy and the big collie bringing up

the rear of the procession, she lost her smile.

Ruth was quick to notice that Meta wasn't pleased to see the big dog that had frightened her. She told Timmy, "Timmy boy, there's no sense in your bringing Lassie into the house. Why don't you take her for a little walk, and then wait in the car?"

"But I want to see Letty! An' Lassie wants to see Pom-Pom!" Timmy protested.

"Letty's in the barn with her pony," Dave Brunson told him quickly, "and Pom-Pom's sure to be there, too."

"Mom, why can't we go see them?" Timmy coaxed.

Ruth looked at Meta and waited for her to speak. Meta hesitated a moment, then she nodded reluctantly.

"All right," Ruth told him sternly, "but don't forget your manners! And don't play too rough. Remember, Letty's only a little girl, not as strong as Boomer is!"

"Okay, Mom! We'll remember!" And he and Lassie tried to outrun each other to the barn.

The barn looked a lot different from the last time he had been inside it. That was when he had been looking for a rope to help get the stranger out of the well. Instead of being all dust and cobwebs, and smelly from old moldy hay, it had been swept clean.

And there in a stall stood the cutest little fat brown Shetland pony, with a real star-shaped blaze on its forehead. Timmy gasped, "Golly!" Lassie cocked her head on one side and sniffed inquiringly.

But Timmy didn't see anything of Letty, though he looked around the barn for her and even went out behind the barn and into the field beyond.

Then he came back in again, with Lassie tagging at his heels. "Guess she's some place else," he told Lassie. And Lassie barked and sniffed the air inquiringly, as if she knew he was looking for someone, and wanted to help him. "I give up," he admitted, and started to wander toward the front doors, still looking hopefully into corners.

But he hadn't looked in the right place for Letty. She had seen him running toward the barn, and had hastily climbed up into the loft, carrying the wiggling Pom-Pom under one arm. Now both were lying flat on the rough flooring, peering down excitedly at the visitor.

"Hi, Letty! Where are you?" Timmy yelled. "It's me an' Lassie!" And when there was no answer, he gave up.

But just then a large bright-colored rubber ball bounced down out of the hayloft and bumped across the floor, just missing him. There was a loud giggle from the hayloft, and an excited yipping from Pom-Pom mixed in with it.

Timmy located the giggle. "Hey! Who you tryin' to knock down?" he demanded angrily.

A pert little face framed in yellow curls showed over the edge of the hayloft. "I could'a hit you if I wanted to!" it announced. "I'm a good thrower." A small nose wrinkled at him.

"Huh!" Timmy wrinkled his own nose in reply. "Girls can't throw!"

"Well, *I* can!" Now she was getting annoyed. "And I can ride a pony! And *you* can't!"

"Could if I tried!" Timmy yelled back. He swaggered in the direction of the pony's stall. "I'll show you!"

"You keep away from Taffy!" Letty shrieked. "He bites when strangers touch him!"

"Yah!" Timmy hooted. "Ponies don't bite! They're tame!"

Two small legs in jeans swung out of the hayloft and Letty was suddenly down the ladder and running toward the pony's stall. "Don't touch him!" she called. "Keep back!"

10
THE QUARREL

But before Letty could get to the pony's stall to stop Timmy, he had gone boldly up to the mild-eyed brown head that was hanging over the top plank of the stall, and was reaching out to stroke the pony's nose.

Apparently this was what Taffy had been waiting for. There was a sudden swift movement, as the pony jerked its head away, with bared teeth. Then it took a vicious nip at Timmy's arm. It all happened so quickly that Timmy had no chance to pull back out of danger.

But Lassie had come up with Timmy and was watching uneasily. As the pony struck, Lassie leaped against Timmy, and knocked him out of the way. The pony's strong teeth missed the flesh of Timmy's arm, but closed with a loud snap on the sleeve of his shirt, ripping it half off.

Knocked off balance by the weight of Lassie's body, Timmy staggered sideways, tripped, and fell into an opened bale of hay.

For a moment, the breath was knocked out of him. Then he sat up, looking around with a surprised expression. There was hay sticking to his hair and clothes.

Letty took one look and turned away, covering her eyes with her arm.

Timmy saw her shoulders shaking, and thought she was crying. "What are *you* crying for?" he demanded crossly. "It was me your mean ol' pony tried to bite!"

Letty took her arm down and turned around, and Timmy discovered that she wasn't crying at all. She was laughing. And she kept on laughing. At *him!* "You—looked so funny —fallin' into the hay!" she gasped.

Timmy scowled at her. He got up, brushing off the hay. "Come on, Lassie. Let's get out of here." And he led Lassie toward the door. "Some people have no manners!"

Letty sobered instantly. "Aw, please! Don't be mad!" She hurried after him. "I didn't mean to laugh at you, Timmy. But you were so—cute—tumblin' over."

But Timmy's scowl stayed on, and he marched toward the door. Cute! No girl was going to call him "cute"!

But he made the mistake of looking back when he got as far as the door. She was standing, looking sad, with her thumb in her mouth and two genuine tears rolling down her cheeks as she watched him go.

"Okay!" Timmy gave up. "I guess you couldn't help it. I guess I did look funny."

Letty dashed away the tears and ran to him. "Come on! I'll inter-duce you and Taffy. He's a doll when he knows you!"

So Timmy let himself be led back toward the stall, though Lassie stood aside, whining protestingly.

"This is a new friend, Taffy," Letty said solemnly. "He likes ponies. You must never try to bite him again!"

So Taffy, resting his chin on her shoulder, waggled his ears at Timmy, and even allowed him to scratch one of them.

"Timmy! We're going soon!" It was his dad's voice.

"All right, Dad!" Timmy called back. Then he pointed to the pony. "Do you s'pose I could ride him sometime?"

"Sure! It's easy as pie. I'll show you how," she promised, "next time I see you!" She beamed at him. "When are you and Lassie comin' over again?"

"Real soon," Timmy promised. Then as Lassie tugged at his sleeve and pulled him toward the door, "So long!"

And Letty, climbing the hayloft ladder again to rescue a loudly indignant poodle pup, confided happily to it, "We'll have lots of fun this summer, Pom-Pom. You, and me, and Taffy! And Timmy and Lassie!"

She gave him a hug and climbed down with him, to run after Timmy.

Dave Brunson and Paul had left the two mothers to get acquainted over a cup of tea, while they took a stroll around the property. Paul didn't hesitate to tell Dave Brunson how much he envied him the fine piece of land. "Once you get the hang of farming," he told Dave, "you should make a good living here. It's the best soil in the township."

"Do you really think so?" Dave asked eagerly.

Paul took a handful of the damp dirt, and crumbled it between his fingers. "Rich! You should have bumper crops."

Dave made a grim face. "I suppose anybody with a little know-how would! But I'm just a greenhorn. I can't even keep the seed in the ground! Look at that field! It's one big mud puddle!"

"You can't blame yourself for the weather!" Paul smiled at his neighbor. "That puddle ought to be dried off in a couple of days, and the ground will be just right for working!"

"I'd better start arranging to get that horse again, and a new supply of seed!" Dave looked glum.

"Tell you what!" Paul pretended the thought had just occurred to him, "Why don't you use our tractor? It would get the work done in half the time!"

"I'm sorry—I can't afford to rent it. I'm—a bit short of ready cash," Dave said honestly.

"Who said anything about renting?" Paul grinned. "We still have one field to plow and sow. After that, the big gas eater will be just standing around till harvest. You might as well use it!"

Dave's eyes lighted up. Then he shook his head slowly. "Thanks, but I don't believe in borrowing."

Paul was silent a moment. Then he put his hand on Dave Brunson's shoulder and said, "I'm sorry you feel that way, Dave. Around here, we don't consider it a disgrace for a man to borrow his neighbor's tools, so long as he takes good care of them. And if a man is too proud to borrow them, we naturally have to judge that *he* wouldn't lend his own tools to someone who needed them."

"If I had anything worth lending you in return," Dave answered, "it would be different! But the way it looks now, I'm licked before I start!"

"Dave!" It was Meta's voice, and as Dave turned in surprise at the happy tone of it, he saw her and Ruth hurrying toward them from the house. Meta's face was radiant. She looked happier than he had seen her since they had come here. "Wait till you hear what we've been planning!"

Ruth was smiling, too. She stopped to put an arm over Timmy's shoulders as he and Lassie came up to her, and put the other arm over Letty's shoulders as they walked along together, both youngsters chattering eagerly.

"When we go over to get the tractor," Meta told her husband gaily, "Mrs. Martin is going to lend us a round maple table that matches our kitchen chairs. It'll just fit in the kitchen by the window!"

Dave looked startled. Paul caught his eye and grinned.

"The boys can tie it on the back of your car," Ruth told her, laughing. "And they'd better tie it on tight, or it'll fall off and get smashed into kindling when Dave comes along behind you in the tractor!"

"I'll strangle him if that happens!" Meta giggled. "You

saw how much furniture we have!"

Dave looked at Paul and Paul looked at him, and Dave made a gesture of resignation. It seemed that the ladies had settled the borrowing question! All he could do now was to go along with it.

"I'll send Timmy over on his bike as soon as we get the seed in," Paul promised. "Should be in a couple of days."

On the way home, Paul teased Ruth about getting so well acquainted with Meta Brunson at their first meeting. "How did you do it?" he grinned. "Dave told me she didn't make friends easily, and was here sort of against her wishes just for Letty's health."

"Oh, I don't know. I liked her right away. And I've always believed that if you like someone, really like them, they're bound to feel it, and they can't help being friendly. I'm sure we'll get along fine, all of us." Ruth smiled confidently. "They're both nice. And little Letty is a darling."

She turned to speak to Timmy in the back seat, cuddled against Lassie. "I hope you played nicely—" she broke off, surprised—"how did you get your sleeve so torn?"

Timmy hesitated. There was no use tattling on the pony, now that they were going to be good friends. Mom might forbid him to learn to ride it. So he said, truthfully, "It got torn while I was out in the barn."

Ruth sighed. "A nail, I suppose. Well, you'll just have
to wear it mended. I wish you'd be more careful."

Timmy nodded vigorously. "Yes'm, I sure will." And
he sighed with relief as she turned around and started talking to Dad again. But Lassie looked up at him and whined,
and Timmy whispered in her ear, "Sh-h-h! You *know* I
couldn't tell her! But I didn't fib, really!"

The next day, Uncle Petrie and Paul plowed the south
field. The new tractor performed like a champion, and the
work was finished in just a few hours. Then there was
only the sowing of the seed to do, and that wouldn't take
long, either.

Timmy and Lassie watched for a while, and Timmy had
a couple of rides on the tractor, with Lassie running along-
side and keeping up a steady barking. It was great fun for
both of them, but Paul finally got tired of the noise and
shooed them away.

Timmy sauntered back to the yard, and he and Lassie
sat outside the barn. He didn't feel like bicycling over to
Boomer's house. Boomer was still busy with that silly
chicken coop. Spring vacation was nice, for a day or so, but
it got pretty boring after that. School wasn't so bad, after

all. There was always something interesting going on.

There was a lot of stir and bustle inside the house today. Mom was engaged in a mysterious something called spring cleaning. It meant that all the furniture had to be moved, and the curtains taken down. And the vacuum cleaner was going for hours. And after it was all done, it didn't look any different to Timmy and the other two male members of the household, than before it all started. But it seemed to be something that happened at everybody's house, and it had to be endured.

The telephone was ringing. Mom's voice answered it and a couple of minutes later, she called him.

"Boomer's mom has started her spring cleaning, too. How would you like to take Lassie and meet Boomer at the creek? She's packed him a lunch, and I can fix one for you, too."

Timmy's eyes brightened. Maybe if they started right away, they would have time to go to the cave and see the old man again! "Golly, Mom! That would be swell. But —don't bother about fixin' my lunch. I can do it myself."

"That's a good idea! I'll just keep on with my work. Take whatever looks good to you!" Ruth told him.

It took only a few minutes for Timmy to fill his lunchbox, but when he got through, it was just about the heaviest lunch box in history. And the cold roast in the icebox looked like a skeleton of its former plump self. In addition to the lunch box full of sandwiches and cake, Timmy stowed a couple of apples in his pockets and a handful of last night's biscuits inside his shirt. His friend at the cave was going to have plenty of crumbs for the birds and the deer.

Boomer was under their special tree beside the creek when Timmy and Lassie got there. He had his fishing line in the water, and was leaning against the tree with his hands clasped behind his head and his eyes closed.

Timmy was panting. That heavy lunch box and his fishing pole weighed more than he had counted on.

He threw himself down on the soft grass beside Boomer. "Whew!" He rubbed a sleeve over his perspiring face. "Thought I'd never get here!"

Boomer opened his eyes and yawned. His fishing cork was still bobbing idly on top of the water. He looked at Timmy and frowned. "What'cha got inside your shirt?"

"Biscuits for the deer, an' the other wild animals at the cave," Timmy boasted, and pulled one out to display it. "I got apples, too. And meat and stuff. I bet Joey'll be glad to see us."

"Yeah, if he hasn't got scared an' run off!"

Timmy looked worried. "But he said he'd stay a few days! And we promised to come back. He wouldn't just leave, without telling us."

"He would, too," Boomer looked scornful. "He's only a tramp, no matter what he told you! An' my pa says tramps are no good. They steal an'—"

"Not Joey! An' he's not a tramp! He's a nice ol' man, an' I betcha he's still in the cave! An' I'm goin' to see! You can stay here if you want to!"

Boomer scowled. "That's just what I'm going to do! He's a dirty ol' tramp!" He shouted angrily, and got to his feet, doubling his fists. "I hope he's gone an' he never comes back!"

"He's not a dirty ol' tramp! You take that back!" Timmy doubled up his own fists and shook them at Boomer.

"He is too! He is too!" Boomer yelled.

Lassie looked surprised and puzzled. This was a new game they were playing and she didn't like it. But something moved in the brush, and she was instantly on guard.

11

TRICKY TAFFY

Lassie stared hard at the spot in the brush where the noise she had heard was coming from. But instead of growling, she gave a little whine and wagged her tail.

Both boys heard the whine, and looked to see what had caused it. Their quarrel was forgotten as a small white puppy came pushing out of the bushes and romped toward Lassie.

"Pom-Pom!" Timmy exclaimed, glad to see the small poodle again. "Whatcha doin' here?" and he hurried over to pet the visitor.

But Pom-Pom was much more interested in saying hello to his friend Lassie than in greeting the boys. He gave

Timmy and Boomer a quick waggle of his plumed tail, and then proceeded happily to maul Lassie's ears again.

Lassie put her head down and covered her ears with her paws. Which baffled the poodle, and made both the boys laugh heartily.

The poodle pup sat down, his head tilted, to study the problem of getting at Lassie's ears again. But Lassie kept them covered. So he gave up and made a quick run toward her slowly waving tail. Lassie knew what to expect, and she hastily tucked the tail under a hind leg. But the tip still stuck out, and the poodle made a wild pounce on it, grabbed it, and tried to back off with it in his teeth.

Lassie had had enough. She stood up suddenly, switched her tail and sent the pup tumbling head over heels.

It sat up whimpering and shaking itself. But it wasn't hurt, and a moment later it was back chewing at Lassie's whiskers.

Both boys were laughing so hard at the two dogs that they didn't notice that Letty had ridden in along the woods path on Taffy. It was only when she started laughing with them, that they noticed her. They were both startled.

"Hi!" she greeted them. "I heard you laughing! Pom-Pom's cute, isn't he?"

"He's a pest!" Boomer said promptly, with a scowl. "Serve him right if Lassie beat him up!"

Timmy saw Letty's frightened look, and told her quickly, "Boomer's only fooling. Lassie likes Pom-Pom!"

Letty's face cleared. She smiled at Timmy, and assured him, "I wasn't scared. Lassie's our friend." She threw a disapproving look toward Boomer. "Some people are silly."

Boomer's face got red and he stuck out his jaw and scowled at her. "We don't want any girls hangin' around. This is our special place."

Letty tossed her head. She deliberately got down from Taffy's back. "Who says so?" she challenged.

"Me—an' Timmy," Boomer snapped.

Letty turned her shoulder to him, and smiled sweetly at Timmy. "If you want to, I'll let you ride Taffy," she told him. "I'll show you how to get on."

"Yah! Who wants to ride an ol' pony?" Boomer sneered. "Go on away!"

"I don't have to. Do I, Timmy?"

Timmy was already on his way up to her and Taffy. He shook his head. "Nope!"

Boomer was shocked at his desertion. For a moment he was speechless.

"I'll hold Taffy's bridle," Letty told Timmy. "Put your foot in that stirrup and pull yourself up." And as Timmy obeyed, she continued, "Now throw your other leg over the saddle an' sit down quick."

Boomer stood glaring at his faithless friend as Timmy followed instructions.

"Hey! I did it!" Timmy said happily to Letty.

"Here are the reins." She handed them up to him and Timmy took them clumsily. "Hold 'em tight."

"Now what do I do?" he asked, a little shakily.

"Ride 'im, cowboy!" Boomer yelled suddenly.

Taffy snorted, threw back his head, and took off at a fast clip, almost unseating Timmy with his first leap. Letty screamed and backed away, and Timmy dropped the reins and grabbed the runaway pony around the neck in a desperate effort to stay on.

In a moment, they had almost gone out of sight along the creek bank, crashing through bushes, narrowly missing trees. Timmy, yelling with fright, hung on somehow.

Boomer, horrified at what he had done, could only stare after them, open-mouthed.

But after the first moment of surprise, Lassie was on her feet and streaking after the runaway as fast as she could go.

A low branch just missed Timmy's head, as he cowered on the pony's back and tried frantically to hold on. He was yelling, "Stop! Whoa! Stop!"

Now his right foot had slipped out of the stirrup, and as Taffy ran at top speed through the tangle of willows along the creek, Timmy started to slide sideways out of the saddle. In a couple more minutes, he would be so far off balance that he would tumble to the ground.

But now Lassie was catching up with them. And Timmy heard her bark, close behind him. He sobbed with relief. "Lassie!" He didn't know how she was going to stop the runaway pony, but some of his terror left him. He tugged hard at the flying mane, yelling, "Whoa! Whoa!" but the pony just snorted and kept going.

Lassie had caught up with them now, and was running neck and neck with the frightened pony. Now she leaped at one of the dangling reins and caught it in her teeth. She hung on, and was dragged a dozen feet before the weight of her body gradually slowed down the runaway, and finally brought him to a stop.

Timmy slid out of the saddle and collapsed in a heap on the ground, dazed, shaken, and almost in tears.

Lassie dropped the rein and came limping back to sniff

inquiringly at him. Timmy slipped his arm around her, and leaned against her soft shoulder. "Th-thank you, girl."

And a couple of minutes afterward, when Letty and Boomer came stumbling after him, white-faced and scared, he was still sitting with his arm around Lassie.

They found Taffy a few feet away, calmly munching some fresh green grass and acting as if nothing at all had happened.

"Are you all right?" Boomer dropped down beside his pal.

Timmy nodded without answering.

"Golly, I'm sorry I scared him. I was just tryin' to be funny," Boomer said miserably.

"It's all right," Timmy blinked back a betraying tear. "Lassie made him stop runnin'. An' I didn't fall off." He managed a grin at his pal, and Boomer found one to give back.

"Try it again. I won't make any noise this time," Boomer suggested. "You can ride him okay."

Timmy shook his head. "I think I'll wait till some other day. I don't feel much like it now."

"You're not mad at Taffy, are you?" Letty asked anxiously. "He didn't mean to run away. He likes you."

"I'm not mad, honest. He's a fine little pony. An' I like him. It's only. . . ." Timmy squirmed uneasily.

"We gotta go see a friend of ours," Boomer put in importantly. "An' we can't waste any more time."

Timmy looked surprised. "I thought you said—" he began.

Boomer interrupted. "Come on. Let's pick up the lunch an' get started. He'll be lookin' for us." And he beckoned Timmy to come along with him as he turned and started back toward their fishing spot.

"Can't I go, too?" Letty asked Timmy eagerly.

But Timmy dug one toe in the ground and shook his head solemnly. "I'm sorry," he told her, "it's a secret. Just me an' Boomer an' Lassie."

Letty's eyes flashed. "Pooh! Keep your old secret!" she told him witheringly. "I wouldn't go if you *begged* me!" She stalked toward her pony.

Timmy looked sad. He didn't want to make anybody angry. But today, everybody was getting mad at him. He tried for a moment to think of something to say to Letty, but he couldn't. So he turned and dashed off through the woods after Boomer. Lassie ran at his heels. She had lost her limp, and except for a couple of places where the rocks had scraped off a little hair on her leg, she was fine.

Letty watched them disappear. Then she put her face down on her saddle and wailed, "I hate boys! They're all mean! I hate them!"

Timmy and Boomer tramped through the woods toward the old cave, carrying the lunch boxes and their fishing poles.

"You don't have to come if you don't want to," Timmy reminded his friend.

"I know it!" Boomer scowled. "An' I wouldn't go, just to see that ol' tramp. But I want to see the animals."

Timmy nodded happily. He was glad to have Boomer along on any terms. Weren't they best friends?

Long before they came in sight of the cave, old Joey knew he was going to have company. The squirrel he had been feeding suddenly stopped eating and, with a frightened chattering, fled up into the tree. And the robin that had been hopping about the ground a few feet away, searching for worms, its head cocked over a plump orange breast, flew up suddenly and was gone into the sky.

And just as suddenly, Joey had slipped into the cave, carrying the few bits of bread that he had been eating before he had stopped to coax the squirrel over.

Just inside, in the shadows, he waited tensely for the first sound that might let him know who the visitors were. But suddenly he relaxed. The two young voices that he was hearing were the voices of his two little friends who had promised to come back and see him. He wondered if they had remembered to bring some crumbs for the birds.

He sat down outside the cave and waited for them. In a moment, Lassie bounded up, with the boys a few yards behind her. She sat down beside old Joey, put a paw on his lap, and offered her silky ear to be scratched.

Boomer was friendlier today. He was trying to be extra nice because he still felt guilty about causing the runaway. He even offered to share his lunch with Joey, but Timmy had brought such a load of things that there was no need of any more.

Timmy was feeling fine, and inclined to look back now at the runaway as quite a funny happening. He proudly told how Lassie had stopped the pony "—just when I was fallin' off!"

Joey nodded wisely. "Lucky she was there, son! I recollect, I bought a pony for my boy once—" He stopped abruptly, and passed his hand across his eyes.

"You did?" Timmy asked, puzzled at the sudden end of

Joey's story. "Did *it* run away, too?"

Joey looked at him blankly. "I don't remember. I—" He paused. Then he shook his head sadly and told them, "It's gone again. For a minute, I almost remembered. . . ."

The boys exchanged sympathetic looks. Timmy spoke up soberly, "Don't worry, Mister Joey. It'll all come back, someday."

"Sure it will!" Boomer added hastily. Then, because he felt uncomfortable, he asked abruptly, "Where's the wild animals?"

Joey looked startled. "The wild—*animals?*"

Timmy threw a reproving look at Boomer, and then explained politely, "He means he'd like to see some of your pets you told us you'd show us."

"Oh!" Joey grinned. His momentary distress had vanished. "Now you just sit tight, both of you, and Lassie too. And we'll see who's around right now."

Lassie seemed to understand. She lay motionless, while Joey pursed his lips and whistled a few soft notes. They held their breath, waiting, but nothing happened. Then Joey whistled again, a little louder and sort of coaxing.

And from only a few feet away, in the brush, a robin began singing. The boys grinned happily, but one of Lassie's

ears twitched. And the singing stopped abruptly.

"Keep still, Lassie!" Timmy whispered. "You'll scare him away!"

There was a flutter of wings, and a cocky bird with a bright blue jacket and a handsome crested head landed only a couple of feet from Lassie's black nose. He strutted about importantly, almost as if he were daring the collie to start something. And when old Joey scattered some biscuit crumbs in his direction, the impudent bluejay hopped around picking them up, but not hurrying in the least. He swallowed the first two or three, and then filled his beak with the largest that were left. After which he made a gurgling noise in his throat, and took off, a bright flash of color that sped right past their faces.

"Goodness! He's not a bit scared of Lassie or us!" Timmy chuckled. "He's sure brave!"

Boomer threw out a handful of crumbs. "Maybe the robin will come back now!"

But Joey looked up at the sky as a sudden raucous cawing broke the silence. He pointed toward a high branch of a tall elm. "Not while that big black fellow's around! He's the boss!"

The boys squinted up eagerly. A large black crow was

up there, watching them. "Caw! Caw!" he remarked.

Boomer picked up a stone, and drew back his arm to heave it up at the crow. But before he could let go of it, the crow had flown away, and they heard his croaking get farther away by the second. Boomer dropped the stone. "Good thing for him he flew away. I'd have hit him spang in the head if he hadn't!"

Timmy felt pretty sure he wouldn't have come anywhere near hitting the crow, but he kept quiet. He had had enough arguments with Boomer today. So he just nodded and tried not to look as if he had any doubts.

Pink clouds were floating across the sky above the trees. That meant that the sun must be pretty low. Timmy scrambled to his feet. "I guess we oughta get on home," he suggested. "Maybe we'll see the animals next time."

So in a few minutes, they were on their way back to the creek, and it wasn't till they were halfway home that Boomer noticed that Timmy had left his fishing pole behind at the cave.

Timmy had forgotten all about it. "Golly! We better go back and get it," he told Boomer.

"It'd be dark before we got home," Boomer objected. "My pa would spank me."

"Well, *I'm* goin'! I'll run all the way," Timmy announced boldly, "an' I bet I get home before dark."

"Go ahead," Boomer told him coldly. "But I bet you don't get *this* far before it gets dark! Well—so long!" He turned away and tramped out of sight with his own fishing pole safely over his shoulder.

Timmy stood with his hand on Lassie's ruff, looking after his friend. Then he looked back toward the darkening woods out of which they had just come. "Come on, Lassie. We'll hurry both ways," he told her, a little shakily.

But Lassie stood where she was and made no move to go along with her small boss. He took a few steps, and then looked back. "You comin', Lassie?" he demanded.

Lassie barked sharply, but stayed where she was. Quite obviously, she had no intention of going back to the cave. And from the tone of her bark, she didn't approve of his going, either.

"Aw, Lassie! I *got* to get my fish pole!" he pleaded. But the shadows were heavy now in the direction of the cave, and somewhere up out of sight in the green branches, an owl had started to hoot mournfully. "Hoo-hoo," it called, "hoo-hoo!" It was just plain spooky.

For a moment more, Timmy hesitated. Lassie stood firm.

Then Timmy came back slowly to her. "Okay, Lassie. We'll go home. But I sure think Mom is going to be awful mad when she finds out I left my pole an' my new reel someplace."

Lassie nudged his hand with her nose, and whined happily as they started along home. Then she ran ahead a few steps, and back to him again, barking. "Hurry up," she seemed to be saying, "and don't change your mind again!"

So they kept on, and got home safely before Mom had had time to worry. But Timmy, washing up for supper, whispered to Lassie, "I kinda wish you hadn't made me come home. I still think I could have got there an' back by dark."

But it was a good thing that he hadn't gone back to the cave. Because old Joey had another visitor now, a most unwelcome one.

12

THE UNWELCOME
GUEST

The two boys and Lassie had hardly disappeared in the woods, when old Joey saw his friend the doe come through the brush, with her fawn close beside her.

He coaxed them over with a handful of the new grass that was growing close to the mouth of the cave. It was a pretty sight to see them moving gracefully about, without fear. He wished that the boys could still have been there to watch.

But after only a few minutes of browsing, the mother deer suddenly lifted her head, sniffed suspiciously, and then bounded away in long, graceful leaps. And the fawn ran off close on her heels.

Now he heard what had alarmed them. It was the sound of someone coming through the brush. For a moment, he thought that it might be the boys, coming back for the rod and reel that Timmy had left standing against the rocks beside the cave entrance.

But he decided quickly that it was someone or something else, because the sound was coming from the opposite direction.

It might be the law, catching up with him at last!

Joey snatched up the fishing pole and tossed it inside the cave. Then he hastily picked up what was left of the picnic lunch, and started into the cave with it.

He hadn't quite gotten out of sight, before a man's gruff voice called out, "Hey, you there! Where d'ya think you're goin'?" and then, "Get your hands up!"

Joey turned slowly, the remnants of the food dropping from his hands as he raised them. But it was no shiny-badged law officer who stood watching him. It was a tall, gaunt man in ragged cotton clothes and wearing a thick beard and shaggy, uncut hair. His small black eyes were set close together under heavy brows, and there was the look of a hunted animal in them. He had a long-nosed revolver in his right hand. And it was leveled at Joey.

As Joey stared, his hands still at shoulder height, the big man strode forward, his eyes fixed on Joey suspiciously. But the old man was so obviously frightened that the intruder decided he was harmless. He came up to him, turned him around, and felt quickly for a revolver in Joey's pockets. Not finding one, he stuck his own gun into his belt and told Joey, carelessly, "You can put down the mitts, gran'pa! I ain't aiming to hurt ya, long as you do like I say!"

Joey lowered his hands slowly, but his eyes still mirrored his fear. "Y-yes, sir," he stammered.

The big man demanded suddenly, "Anybody staying here besides you?" He was looking around suspiciously. "Where'd them sandwiches and all that meat come from? And biscuits!"

Joey explained hurriedly, "Coupla little boys come by. That was their lunch. But they're gone now."

"Good thing I didn't run into them." The dark man looked mean. "I don't like gabby kids."

"They won't be back. Maybe not for days," Joey said quickly. "Days and days. Maybe not at all!"

"That's fine! I figure to take myself a little rest for a few days. I been traveling considerable, lately." The man gave a short, harsh laugh.

"Cave's pretty damp, mister." Joey wanted to discourage his unwelcome guest.

"I can stand it, I reckon. It's bound to beat sleeping out in the open!" He saw through Joey's attempt to discourage him, and a crooked grin made his cruel mouth look even meaner. "So save your breath, old-timer! You got company, like it or not! And don't try to sneak off and hunt up the law!"

"Never had such an idea," Joey told him quietly. "The law's no friend of mine."

The black-bearded man studied him. "Yeah. Well, don't get any notions about trying to square your own self by turning me in."

"Not likely," old Joey shook his head wearily, "even if you didn't have that gun."

The big man seemed convinced. "Now, s'pose you stir around and see what kinda supper you can scare up? I'm almighty hungry."

And when Joey had managed to put together a sort of a meal, of odds and ends of the lunch and a couple of biscuits that he had made with the last of his flour, the big man ate hungrily and wanted more.

"Got nothing more," Joey told him. "Maybe tomorrow

I can catch a fish or two, though."

"Fish?" The black-haired man scowled. "That don't tickle my fancy none. A rabbit's more to my taste. You got a trap in that cave we could use?"

Joey caught his breath. A trap for his friendly little animals! "A what?" he asked, looking blank. He was stalling for time, hoping desperately to think of some way to keep the stranger from rigging up a snare.

"A *trap,* old-timer! Something to catch a meal in!" The big man looked disgusted at Joey's stupidity.

"Oh, a trap!" Joey looked vague. "Nope. None in there when I came, and I got no money to buy one, even if I could take a chance on being seen in town to do it!"

The bearded man shrugged. "Then I guess it's fish tomorrow. But we'll figure some way to get us some good red meat after that!"

Long after the intruder was snoring in the recesses of the deep cave, old Joey squatted by the embers of his fire. He could gather up his small possessions and sneak off during the night. That would rid him of the unwelcome guest. But if he did, where would he go to hide?

He hoped that the big man would get tired of the cave in a day or so, and would go on his way. But most of all he hoped that the two boys and Lassie wouldn't come back till the stranger was gone.

Toward dawn, he took Timmy's fish pole and went to the brook that wound its way through the heavy brush and down into the big creek. Before the first rays of the sun had lightened the sky, he had two plump yellow perch that should make a tasty breakfast for his visitor.

As he made his way back to the cave, he hurried his steps. Every morning, while he ate his own breakfast, he could be sure of an attentive audience. Sometimes it was only the brown and gray squirrel who came to chatter at him till he divided some of his small store with it. Sometimes the robin came and sang at him for crumbs. And sometimes both of them were there, with the bluejay who added his own idea of begging for breakfast. They were all so tame that they wouldn't know that his unwelcome guest might harm them—especially the friendly squirrel.

Sure enough, the squirrel was there waiting. He ran up a tree trunk and skittered out to the end of a branch just over old Joey's head. He made coaxing noises, and got ready to leap down onto Joey's shoulder.

But just then, Joey heard the black-bearded man stirring inside the cave, yawning loudly.

"Shoo!" Joey whispered, and waved his arm threateningly at the squirrel. "Get away from here quick, boy!" The surprised squirrel made a flying leap away from the waving arm, and scampered up into the high branches, scolding as he went. Old Joey watched him leap from one tree to the other till his noisy reproaches were faint in the distance. "Sorry I had to scare you," Joey whispered after his friend, "but you're better off staying away till he's gone!"

But the bearded man had no intention of going. He liked it there.

"Long as I aim to stick around awhile," he told Joey after breakfast, "we might as well get acquainted. What do I call you?"

Old Joey hesitated. If he told the stranger that he was the escaped convict Blackie Sanders, there was a good chance that the visitor would turn him in to the police for the reward. So he told him, "Just Joey."

"Joey, hey?" The black-haired man laughed. "Okay, pop. Joey it is! And you can call me Blondy!"

"Blondy?" Joey looked surprised.

"Yeah! Blondy!" the big man chuckled. "On account of I got yeller hair!" He pulled his jet black beard and laughed heartily at his own joke.

But when Joey didn't join in the laugh, the black-haired man scowled suddenly, and gripped Joey's wrist in his powerful fingers. His lip curled back over his big white animal-like teeth as he snarled, "Got any objections, old-timer?"

Joey cringed. He shook his head dumbly, and his eyes showed such fear that the big man let go of him and gave a contemptuous laugh.

"Okay. Joey and Blondy. That's good enough. And seeing that we're rooming together for a while, let's figure how to get ourselves fixed comfortable here."

"It's not much of a place," Joey said timidly. "And you don't like fish every meal, like I do."

"Leave it to me," the man who called himself Blondy told Joey. "What I don't like, I change."

And beyond that, he told Joey none of his plans. But after another meal of fish, at sundown, he began to make preparations of a sort that worried Joey. He carefully checked the big revolver that he carried in his belt, as if to be sure that it was ready for use. Then he paced the ground in front of the cave and waited impatiently for darkness to set in.

"You going some place?" Joey asked hopefully.

"Yeah. But I'm coming back. So don't figure you got rid of me. And don't try to run off. Your cooking's a heap better'n I can do. And I like somebody to talk to, even if he's a loony old guy like you! Savvy?"

Joey nodded. He wouldn't try to run away. Even if he had someplace to run to, there was something about the black-browed man that struck terror into his hazy mind.

It was well after midnight when Deputy Terry, making his rounds, noticed that the front door of Sam Moss's store was standing partly open. In twenty years, that was the first time it hadn't been locked and padlocked.

Gun in hand he made a cautious entrance, but there was no one inside. Someone had broken into the cash register, and it was standing open and empty. All around the store, he saw evidence that the place had been looted.

The deputy woke Sam with a phone call, and then reported to Sheriff Bennett. They were both there within a few minutes.

"It's hard to say what all they got," Sam admitted ruefully, "but there's some choice lamb chops, at a dollar twenty a pound, missing. And half a dozen tenderloin steaks I was saving for the mayor's wife!"

Carl Bennett pointed to the shelves where gaping spaces showed in the orderly arrangement of cans. "With that much stuff gone, I'd guess at least a couple of men were in on the theft. And they probably had a car to carry it off in."

Sam Moss agreed, but Deputy Terry discovered that a sackful of potatoes had been dumped in the storeroom, probably so the thief could pile his loot into the empty burlap bag. "One man could have carried the sackful, but he'd have to be an almighty big feller and strong as an ox!"

They would have been surprised, at that very moment, to see how closely the deputy's description fitted the thief. Big Blondy was staggering up to the cave, the bulging sack slung over his shoulder.

He dumped it at old Joey's feet, and tin cans by the dozen came rolling out.

Joey stared in amazement touched with fear. "Must've weighed near a hundred pounds, and you toted it all the way from town!"

Blondy squared his massive shoulders and grinned. "I sure did, pop! Didn't I tell ya to leave it to me?"

Joey leaned over to examine the contents of the sack. "Meat! And flour! And *cooked* beans!"

Blondy chuckled. "We'll be eating high on the hog for a spell," he boasted. "And when this is all et up, I'll get us some more fancy food!"

He didn't mention the twenty-odd dollars that he had taken out of the cash register, or a certain other thing he had found there. That was his private business, and there was no reason to tell the old man about it.

In the morning, Sheriff Bennett talked it over with his deputies. "I'm betting that it was a couple of tramps from the hobo jungle down by the railroad bridge. Maybe we ought to drop in on them."

But when Bennett and a couple of his men drove over for a quick search of the "jungle" they found no sign of the food. The "jungle" was a tin-can settlement where the hoboes dropped off the freight trains to rest a few hours or a few days between journeys. Its residents changed continually, as some drifted in and others drifted out.

The sheriff and his men found only a few homeless old-timers there. Most of the men were traveling because of the balmy springtime weather. Those who were there knew Sheriff Bennett. Some had spent time in the Calverton jail, as vagrants, and were loudly apologetic for coming back after being ordered out of town.

None of them could remember seeing a big man who could carry a sackful of canned goods. He was most certainly no decent hobo! They were sure of that.

"Well, thanks anyhow, boys," Sheriff Bennett told them. "It may have been some campers who ran out of supplies and money." Then he told them, not unkindly, "You know our law around here. Better be on your way by tomorrow, unless you want to lend a hand painting the jail for a couple of weeks. This is just the weather for painting."

A few minutes later, as he and his two constables rode off in the official red car, he glanced back toward the "jungle" and saw that several of them had already taken his advice and were hotfooting it off down the road, pack on back!

"That's one way to get those 'boes to move on!" Terry grinned. "Threaten them with work!"

They all laughed in agreement. But Sheriff Bennett soon looked thoughtful and serious.

"Where do we look now, boss?" Terry asked. "Do you really think some campers broke in?"

"I don't know what to think," Bennett said glumly. "And I wouldn't know where to start looking!"

13

THE TELLTALE PRINT

Sam Moss ran out into the street to hail the sheriff as the red car moved through Main Street toward the jail.

"Any sign of him?" he asked anxiously.

"Not yet," Bennett told him quickly, "but we haven't given up."

"There's something I want to show you. Didn't notice it last night, in the dark!" Sam Moss was excited. "A footprint!"

The car stopped with a jolt. "Go on to the office," Bennett told his deputies. "See if anything's come in. I'll be along."

Then he hurried around to the rear of the store with Moss. "Look! He spilled some of the flour, and then stepped on it. Look at the size of that shoe print!"

It was huge, all right. Carl Bennett knelt and measured it. "Whew! A whopper!" he said softly.

"Big man, hey?" Sam Moss looked scared. "I'm glad he waited till I was out of the store before he came in! He must be a giant!"

Carl Bennett frowned. He was trying to remember where he had read or heard about some man who wore an over-size shoe.

Suddenly it came to him. "Blackie Sanders!" he exclaimed. "That's where I saw it mentioned! In the Wanted notice for Blackie Sanders!"

"But nobody's seen him around here since that salesman claimed he gave him a lift. And I never did put much stock in *his* story." Sam Moss didn't want to think that the escaped convict was anywhere around Calverton. Neither did Carl Bennett, but he had to face the fact of that unusual footprint!

"Oh!" Sam had suddenly remembered. "There was something I forgot to look for last night." He led the way inside and to the drawer underneath the cash register. "I keep a box of shells for my army revolver in this drawer. They're gone—the whole box!"

Sheriff Bennett looked grim. There could be only one reason for the thief to take those shells. He must have a revolver that they would fit! The rumor was that Sanders had stolen a revolver from one of the guards when he escaped from prison. If he was the thief, he would be doubly dangerous now, with the added ammunition.

"Better not mention around town that we think there's a chance it's Blackie Sanders," he advised the storekeeper. "If it *was* Sanders, he could have been traveling in a stolen car, and be a long way from here by now. No use getting the whole community in an uproar."

"But suppose it *is* Sanders, and he's hiding in some empty house or barn?" Sam Moss's voice shook.

"We'll quietly post the farmers to be on the lookout for him, and to let us know the moment they see anyone that might be Sanders."

So it was that during the next day, Bennett and his men made several visits, singly, to outlying farms. They were careful not to alarm the farmers' families by their questions, but took the menfolk aside each time for private talks.

"Ring us at once, night or day, if you think you've seen him," Bennett told Paul Martin, when he stopped by the south field where Paul and Uncle Petrie were seeding the last row. "And you might warn Brunson."

"You bet we will!" Paul assured him. "Tonight!"

"Might be better not to frighten Ruth and Timmy," Carl Bennett suggested, "though I think I'd keep the youngster out of the woods and close to home for a few days, just in case!"

"Good idea!" Uncle Petrie nodded, then he added soberly, "though Lassie would take care of him if Sanders or anybody raised a hand to hurt the boy!"

"She might try," Bennett said grimly, "but Lassie's teeth wouldn't stand a chance against a revolver. And from Sanders' record, he wouldn't mind using it."

"I'll see that both Timmy and Lassie stay out of his way!" Paul assured his friend firmly.

It was a gay little cavalcade that drove through the gate of the Brunson farm a couple of hours later.

First came Ruth, at the wheel of the sedan, and with the old maple table teetering crazily on top of the car.

Uncle Petrie was leaning half out of the front window, holding onto one leg of the table and shouting every time Ruth hit a bump in the road, "She's topplin'!" But the table continued to stay on top in spite of its wobbling—and it was Uncle Petrie who nearly fell out, not the table!

In the back seat, Timmy and Lassie were thoroughly enjoying the excitement. They didn't mind the bumps in the road. They thought the jostling and bouncing around were a lot of fun.

A dozen yards behind the slow-moving sedan, Paul came rumbling along in the shiny new tractor. He had brought his plow along, too, remembering what he had heard about Dave Brunson having to use the old rusty plow that his father had abandoned twenty years ago.

Dave and Meta Brunson came out to meet their visitors as the sedan stopped, and Letty and Pom-Pom ran in from the barn.

Uncle Petrie climbed out of the car, with shaking knees. "Never thought we'd make it!" He leaned against the door and mopped his brow with his sleeve.

But no sooner were the words out of his mouth, than the table's moorings finally gave 'way, and down it tumbled from the top of the car, missing him by only a few inches as it went by. He made a wild grab, but the table got past him and landed with a crash.

The table wasn't harmed, but Uncle Petrie's feelings were when Ruth laughed. "Mighta brained me!" he grumbled. " 'Tain't funny, Ruth!"

"You sort of brought it on yourself," Ruth giggled, "the way you've been expecting it to fall, for the last two miles!"

Then while Ruth and Meta bossed the job, Uncle Petrie lugged the offending table into the house, grumbling all the way, and Dave hurried down the road to meet Paul and the tractor, his face bright with renewed hope at the sight of it.

Timmy had piled out of the sedan the moment it stopped, and was looking around eagerly for Letty. She came running from the barn, with Pom-Pom at her heels.

"Come see Taffy! I just finished brushing him, an' he looks so pretty!" Letty invited, after the first hellos. Then she looked past him toward the car. "Where's Lassie? Didn't you bring her?"

"Why, sure!" Timmy squinted back at the car. Lassie was still inside, but making no effort to get out. "Come on, Lassie! Here's Pom-Pom!" he called.

But Pom-Pom didn't wait. He ran toward the car as fast as his short little legs could carry him. And, yipping hysterical greetings, he tried to climb inside.

It was too much of a climb. He fell on his back, and ki-yied as if he had been mortally hurt.

Lassie was unmoved. She merely cocked her head to one side and watched the pup scramble to his feet and charge again at the car. Once again he failed to make it, and fell back. Then he sat staring in at her, and whining reproachfully.

"Why doesn't she get out and play with Pom-Pom?" Letty demanded.

" 'Cause she doesn't want her whiskers all chewed again. That's why!" Timmy grinned. "Let's go look at Taffy, an' I betcha Lassie'll be along as soon as Pom-Pom gets over being so glad to see her!"

Taffy was stamping impatiently in the barn, as if he wanted to get out and join the party. He nickered a soft welcome when Timmy and Letty came in, and let Timmy pat his nose and scratch his ear without trying to get in a sly nip.

"He's sorry he ran away with you," Letty explained gravely, "and he's going to be a good pony from now on, forever!" She planted a kiss on the pony's cheek, and Taffy responded by laying his chin on her shoulder and then nuzzling her blond hair. "See what an angel he is?" she asked adoringly.

"Hope he doesn't forget it, next time I try to ride!"

Timmy didn't put too much stock in Taffy's reformation.

"Course he won't!" Letty insisted loyally. "You're his true friend now."

And when Taffy didn't immediately nip him after that, Timmy suggested meeting at the creek tomorrow to try another ride, this time without Boomer to start a runaway.

But when Letty and Timmy reported their plans to their dads a few minutes later beside the tractor, they were met with a flat "No!" from both of them.

"But, Daddy! Why not? You said it was good for me to go riding!" Letty was in tears.

Dave Brunson took her up in his arms, and mopped the tears away gently. "Honey, it's only for a few days. Then you can ride anywhere you want to!"

"But we want to go riding tomorrow!" she wailed, and hid her face on his shoulder, sobbing.

"Timmy is going to stay around home for a few days, too," Paul Martin told her.

Timmy looked astonished. "But I gotta go hikin' tomorrow. I left somethin' important in the woods, an' I got to get it. I'll come right back, soon as I pick it up."

Paul Martin shook his head firmly. "Sorry, son. It'll have

to stay where it is, whatever it is. And don't let's have any arguing about it."

It wasn't often that Dad spoke so sternly to him, so Timmy decided right away that something must really be wrong. He sighed, "Okay, Dad."

But he and Letty both forgot their disappointment when they found out that Timmy and Mom and Dad and Uncle Petrie were all staying for a picnic supper under the cherry tree in the Brunsons' side yard.

Ruth had brought a cake that Mrs. Bates, Boomer's mother, had baked for the new neighbors. And she had added a basketful of cold fried chicken from her own kitchen. So, with some of Mrs. Brunson's own biscuits, and a salad of Martin lettuce, they all had plenty. And the two dogs, side by side and both on their best behavior, came in for their share of thoroughly boned chicken when the feast was over.

Later, when Dave Brunson found a few minutes to talk alone to Paul, he found it hard to say how very grateful he was for the loan of the tractor. "I'm not good at saying thanks," he said quietly, "but I think you know it's going to make the difference between staying here and leaving. And when I see how much better Letty seems since we've been here, even in such a short time, I feel as if things were going to work out the way we've hoped."

"I'm sure they are," Paul agreed heartily. He looked around the yard. "You've really cleaned the place up."

Dave nodded. "There's still plenty to do, but I plan to tackle it a bit at a time, after I get the planting finished."

"It'll be good to see your fields under cultivation," Paul told him with a smile. "I've always envied you this valley. I guess I just couldn't stand seeing it going to waste."

Dave sighed. "They tell me my father had a green thumb, but I'm afraid my fingers are *all* thumbs, and none of them are green!" He laughed ruefully.

"You'll learn by doing, same as the rest of us!" Paul assured him. "But don't hesitate to call, if you need help."

"You've done enough, lending me the tractor! From here on in, I hope I can handle the job without leaning on my neighbors!"

There were only a few things that Paul had to show Dave Brunson about the tractor, and then the Martin family was on its way home.

Timmy was asleep in the back seat, with his head against Uncle Petrie's shoulder and Lassie's head in *his* lap.

Ruth stole a look back at him, to be sure he was sound

asleep. Then she turned to Paul, who was at the wheel. "All right. Now tell me why the children can't go riding tomorrow!"

"Why, uh—" Paul didn't want to worry Ruth. "The—uh—weather bureau says a whopper of a storm is on its way. We don't want them to get caught out in it."

Ruth sighed. "Try again, dear. I heard the broadcast, too. The storm is three or four days away. Now, what is the real answer?" she demanded firmly.

Paul stole a quick look at her. Even in the dim light of the dashboard, he could see she had that look on her face that meant she would keep on asking till he gave her the truth. "Okay. But don't spread it." And he told her about the theft of the food and Bennett's suspicion that it was the escaped convict who had stolen it.

When he had finished, she said quietly, "I hope they find him soon." And a moment later, "I can't help feeling sorry for the poor man, no matter what he's done. It must be dreadful to be hunted, and hungry. He's probably living in constant fear of being caught."

But Ruth Martin was wasting her sympathy. For at that very moment, the man she was pitying was feeling quite at peace with the world. His stomach was full, and he had someone to do the cooking and cleaning up for him, someone to bully, someone who didn't dare disobey his orders on penalty of being cuffed around.

He was sitting beside the fire in the old cave, watching old Joey huddle near the drafty mouth of the cave trying to keep warm without the blanket that his visitor had long since taken for his own use.

The intruder felt like talking. "Hey, old man, what's the law after you for?"

Joey blinked at him sleepily. "Maybe a lot of things. What's it matter?"

"Just passing the time," the big man yawned. The fire was burning low, and he looked around for something to throw on it. The newspaper the boys had brought their sandwiches in was lying near at hand. He picked it up and started to throw it onto the dying fire. Then his eyes caught the headline, and he read the article about the escaped convict Blackie Sanders.

When he had finished, he laid the paper aside again, and looked at the sleeping old man through narrowed, speculative eyes. His hand snaked to the revolver that he had laid aside, and he picked it up and cocked it before he called out, "Hi! Wake up!"

Mumbling protestingly, old Joey turned sleepy eyes on his unwelcome guest. "Wh-what is it now?" he grumbled. Then his eyes popped wide open as he saw the gun in the big man's hand. It wasn't pointing at him, but it could be, at any moment. "Wh-what do you want?"

"You ever hear of Blackie Sanders?" the scowling man asked suddenly.

Joey swallowed hard and nodded, unable to speak.

"There's a nice fat reward for anybody that turns him in, ain't there?" The big man leaned forward, glaring at Joey, his hand toying with the pistol.

"There's no use for the gun, Mister Blondy," the old man said resignedly. "I'll give up without a fight. You got me, fair and square. I admit I'm Sanders!" He held out empty hands, to show that he was unarmed.

The big man's face was in the shadow, but if Joey could have seen it at that moment, he would have seen an expression on it that was a combination of astonishment and disbelief!

14
DISASTER

It took the black-bearded man several seconds to realize that the hazy-minded old fellow really thought that *he* was Blackie Sanders, escaped convict and killer!

And when his slow mind got over the shock, a wide grin spread across his face. Things were working out a lot better than he had expected!

"I don't know how you found out I'm Sanders, but there's no use denying it," the old man said miserably. "My mind's kinda hazy, and I've been sort of hoping I was somebody else, but so long as you know me, that's that."

"Yeah!" The big man nodded, grinning. "You're him, all right. Took me a while to place you, but all of a sudden

I recollected seeing your face in the papers!"

"I suppose you'll be turning me in tomorrow," Joey sighed. "Well, maybe it's just as well. Can't keep on hiding for the rest of my life. Might as well get it over with."

"Who said I figured to turn you in?" Blondy grinned. "I ain't so friendly with the law boys myself. Only" —his grin disappeared suddenly and a scowl took its place "—don't you get any ideas about givin' yourself up! I like it here. So we'll let things ride the way they are—*as long as we get along good!*"

There was a look in his beady black eyes that sent a shiver down Joey's spine. "I didn't have any idea that we wouldn't," he said hastily.

But secretly he wished that Blondy had decided to turn him in and collect the reward. At least he would have been free of his bullying and the constant shadow of that blue-steel revolver.

Lassie came in to wake Timmy up very early the next morning. He was sleepy after being out so late the night before, and tried to hide under the covers. "Go 'way an' let me sleep!" he called out from under the blanket. But

Lassie jumped up on the bed, took the blanket in her teeth, and tugged it off him.

Timmy grabbed for the blanket, but she was too quick for him. She pulled it off the bed and out of his reach.

Then she stood off and barked at him.

"Okay!" Timmy sat up and rubbed his eyes. "Only, there's no school till next week, an' I coulda slept lots longer." But even while he was saying it, he remembered something. "Hey, that's right, Lassie! We're going out to the Brunsons' this morning! Golly! I nearly forgot!"

"Well, Lassie and I didn't forget!" Ruth Martin laughed at him from the doorway. "Hurry up and get washed and dressed. Your breakfast will be ready in five minutes!"

"You bet!" Timmy swung out of bed cheerfully and dashed for the bathroom.

But Ruth caught him by the shoulder as he started to go by her. "Put on your old cords, in case Letty's dad says you may ride Taffy around the yard!" she reminded him.

"Okay!" he grinned up at her. "Golly, we're going to have fun today, aren't we?"

"Of course we are!" Ruth assured him gaily.

And the day started out to be a happy one for both the

Martin family and the Brunsons.

With their planting finished, Uncle Petrie and Paul took time off to go to town and have a talk with Carl Bennett about making up a party to search for Sanders. They went in the pickup truck so Ruth could use the sedan. She had promised to take her portable sewing machine to Meta Brunson, and help make curtains for Meta's kitchen out of some colorful linen dish towels that had been in the bottom of Meta's trunk ever since her wedding. They had been far too pretty to use as towels, but would make gay curtains.

Timmy could hardly wait to arrive at the Brunson farm, and he found Letty and Pom-Pom just as excited as he and Lassie were. Letty's father had left some time ago on the tractor, to start his plowing, but he had made Letty promise not to take the pony away from the farmyard.

"Of course, I won't, Daddy!" Letty had agreed happily.

"That's a good girl!" Dave had stroked her blond head. "In a few days you can ride through the woods again."

He felt pretty sure that the man who had stolen the grocer's meat and canned goods was far away by now, but he felt as Paul and the other farmers did—that there was no use taking chances.

Taffy was tied to the porch rail, and Timmy hadn't the least bit of trouble mounting into the saddle from the steps. He gripped the reins hard at first, but as he got used to the saddle, he relaxed and even urged Taffy to trot.

Letty was delighted, and generously let him ride several times around the yard before she took her turn at riding.

They were having so much fun with Taffy, that for once Timmy forgot all about Lassie being there.

At first, Lassie had watched anxiously as her young owner had mounted into the saddle. She remembered the runaway, and she was alert to the danger. However, when Timmy seemed to have the situation under control, she stretched out in the shade of the maple tree and relaxed. But she kept an eye on the pony just the same.

Pom-Pom had greeted his big friend with the usual ear-nipping, but when she paid less than usual attention to his pestering, he soon got tired of the game. But, puppylike, he couldn't lie down and relax. He had to look for something more exciting to do. His bright eyes followed the pony in its trot around the yard. He seemed to be trying to decide if it would be worth the effort to run after the big brown creature and nip at its heels. But he had done that before, and narrowly escaped being kicked for it. He would have to find something safer to do.

A faint, far-off, familiar sound brought him to his feet, sniffing. A little while ago, he had had a wonderful time barking at that big, slow-moving monster as it clanked its way out of the yard. He had kept after it, doing his best to nip those strange-looking wheels-that-weren't-wheels. And he had won the battle, even without getting in a good bite. It had fled from the yard and down the road.

Now he heard the monster again. He growled threaten-ingly. It wasn't a very ferocious growl, but it was the best he could manage, and it made Lassie sit up and look at him inquiringly.

"Come on!" Pom-Pom barked at Lassie. "Help me drive off the monster!" And then he started off as fast as his legs would take him toward the gate.

Lassie got up slowly. She looked over toward the porch. Timmy and Letty were going to ride double now, and both Mom Martin and Letty's mother were there to show them how. No one seemed interested in what Lassie was doing.

"Come on! Hurry, you slowpoke!" Pom-Pom barked reprovingly. So Lassie trotted slowly toward him, with only one last glance back at Timmy. Then they ran down the road together.

Dave Brunson was rather proud of all the work he had been able to do in one morning with the borrowed tractor. At first, it had seemed an unwieldy monster. But as the morning wore on, he had become quite expert at turning corners and keeping his furrows straight.

In his mind's eye he could already see the tall rows of corn swaying in the summer breezes.

He heard the rippling song of a meadowlark over the sound of the motor, and smiled with happy contentment. This was living! He was beginning to understand why his father had liked farming so well.

Now he heard the far-off yipping of Pom-Pom and with it the deeper barking of Lassie. The Martins must have arrived at the farmhouse. He thought with gratitude what good neighbors they were turning out to be.

Suddenly the barking was closer. Dave didn't pay too much attention to it, until something small and white flashed into sight directly ahead of the tractor. It was Pom-Pom, and apparently he was intent on destroying the strange monster. He was running straight toward it.

"Shoo! Get away! Go, Pom-Pom!" Dave Brunson shouted, waving his arm at the tiny dog in his path. But Pom-Pom kept coming.

Out of the side of his eye he saw Lassie coming at a fast run at an angle, as if she hoped to run the puppy out of the way of the tractor. But she was too far away to help now. There was only one thing to do—swerve the tractor quickly to one side. And even then he couldn't be sure he would miss the tiny white puppy.

He gripped the wheel and swung the tractor over as sharply as he could. But in his panic, he pressed down hard on the gas pedal. The tractor not only swung around, but shot forward in a sudden burst of speed that sent it crashing through the fence and down an embankment into the rock-filled gully beyond.

Dave barely had time to jump from the high seat of the tractor, before it turned over and landed with a crash among the rocks. He fell a few feet from it.

For a moment, he was stunned by his fall. Then he became conscious of a sharp pain in his arm. As he staggered to his feet, he tried to lift the arm and found that he couldn't. It was badly broken.

And the shiny new tractor was smashed and bent so badly that even he, in his ignorance, could see that it would cost a great deal to repair it—*if* it could be repaired.

He felt dizzy, suddenly, and sat down. And when he

tried to get to his feet again, the pain in his arm was so bad that everything went suddenly dark and he pitched forward on his face, in a dead faint.

Up on the edge of the field, Lassie and Pom-Pom stared down at the wreck. Pom-Pom barked hysterically at the fallen monster, but Lassie looked down at the man who was lying motionless a few feet from the tractor.

Then Lassie made a careful descent to Dave Brunson's side. When she got there, she sniffed at him and whined a little, touching him gently with her paw to wake him. When it didn't bring a response, she barked urgently. And when he still lay quiet, she seemed to decide that it was time to do something about it.

She picked up the wide-brimmed straw hat that had fallen off Brunson's head, and with it in her teeth, she climbed up out of the gully and started off at top speed toward the distant farmhouse.

Mrs. Brunson and Ruth Martin had finished the simple little towel curtains, and Ruth was hanging them at the kitchen window, when she saw Lassie come running into the farmyard carrying Dave Brunson's hat in her mouth.

"Now what has that silly dog found?" she laughed, and pointed out the window. "Somebody's hat!"

Timmy and Letty had been sitting on the steps, resting after their pony rides, when they saw Lassie come running into the yard. "Here, girl! Whatcha got?" Timmy called.

But when Lassie brought it over to them, put it down at Timmy's feet, and barked loudly, Letty told Timmy with surprise, "Why, it's Daddy's work hat!"

And at the same time, Meta, staring out of the kitchen window, recognized it also. "She has my husband's hat!" she exclaimed. "How on earth did she get hold of it?"

Ruth watched Lassie run away a few feet, and then come back to bark at Timmy and Letty. She had seen the handsome and intelligent big collie act like that before. She guessed that Lassie was trying to get the children to follow her. Maybe something was wrong . . . . "Let's go see what Lassie's fussing about!" she suggested.

And when the two women came out on the porch, Lassie left the children and ran to them with the hat. She seemed to be glad to see them. She started barking and running back and forth as she had with Timmy and Letty.

"She wants us to go with her someplace!" Timmy ran up. "Can we go, Mom?"

"Why don't we all go?" Ruth suggested quickly. "Maybe Letty's daddy has finished the plowing and sent her to bring us so we can see how nice the field looks!"

So they started out to follow Lassie, who kept running ahead and barking back at them. Long before they came in sight of the empty field with its broken fence, Ruth guessed that there had been some kind of an accident.

She spoke quietly to Meta. "Maybe we'd better keep the children back," she suggested. "I'm afraid something's gone wrong."

But Meta had only one thought, to get to Dave. And she started running across the broken soil, stumbling and almost falling and calling, "Dave! Dave!" as she ran.

Letty immediately broke into loud wails and started to follow her mother, but Ruth caught her and held her back gently but firmly. "Both of you stay right here till we call you. Timmy, take care of Letty—don't let her follow us!"

Then she ran after Meta as fast as she could, confident that she could depend on Timmy. If something tragic had happened to Dave, it was better for Letty not to see it.

But by the time that Meta reached the edge of the field and scrambled down to her husband's side, he was conscious once more, and white-faced with pain from his broken arm. And Pom-Pom, snuggled close to him, was growling defiance at the fallen tractor in the ditch, warning it not to dare make a threatening move or he would tear it to pieces.

Dave managed to stagger to his feet with Meta's help, but he had to lean on her to keep from collapsing. Together they stared at the badly damaged tractor.

"Well, this time I've really done it!" Dave said bitterly. "Smashed myself and Martin's tractor at the same time!"

Ruth spoke as she hurried down to join them. "Don't worry about the tractor. I'm sure it's fully insured against any kind of accident! The important thing is to get you to the doctor right away."

"I hope you're right about the insurance," Dave said miserably a little later, as they all rode in the sedan toward Dr. Wilson's office in Calverton. He was in a great deal of pain, but the damage to the tractor he had borrowed gave him more worry than his own injury.

"Of course, I am!" Ruth called back cheerfully from the front seat. "Paul wouldn't drive any kind of car fifty yards down the street unless it was completely insured. He thinks it isn't fair to other people and it's a foolish risk for the owner!"

Dave Brunson smiled painfully. "I'm lucky that he thinks that way. I hate to think of what it is going to cost to repair that tractor!"

15

DEFEAT

It was a grim-faced group of Calverton men who made a search of the surrounding country to try to find the man who had burglarized Sam Moss's store. Most of them were armed with shotguns, and only the deputies and sheriff had revolvers.

The searchers split into parties of two, and each covered a section of territory. They went into every barn and shed, and searched every empty house. But there was no cache of stolen food to be found, and no trace of the thief.

Twice during the morning, a pair of searchers moved through the deep woods, on their way from one farm to another in a more remote location. And twice, they were watched from deep in the tangled brush by the black-bearded man with a revolver in his belt. He had a very good hunch that they were looking for him, and he was ready to kill rather than be captured. So it was a good thing for them that they had no idea he was close at hand.

He watched them move away and then he went back to the cave to old Joey. Joey was getting ready to go fishing, but Blondy stopped him.

"We got plenty to eat here. I don't want any fish," he told Joey.

"I just thought it might go good," Joey explained. "I'll eat fish, and you can have the steaks."

But Blondy scowled suspiciously and snapped, "You stay right here, old-timer. You ain't fooling me a bit. You figure to follow them lawmen and tell 'em where I am!"

"Lawmen?" Old Joey blinked. "Where?"

Blondy studied him a moment, but Joey's bewilderment convinced him. He relaxed, and even laughed. "Okay, I was just kidding you, pop! There ain't any lawmen. I made it up for laughs! But—no fishing today!"

Joey sighed and set the fishing pole inside the cave. "Had my mouth set for fish, but I guess tomorrow's just as good." And he went inside to start the fire for their next meal.

It was a couple of hours later that Paul Martin, riding in Sam Moss's pickup truck with Uncle Petrie and two more of the searchers, saw his own sedan parked in front of the Calverton Hospital.

In a flash, he was out of the truck and running over to the sedan.

Timmy and Letty were huddled on the back seat with Lassie and Pom-Pom. Letty's face was tear-streaked, but she had gotten over her tears for the moment.

"Timmy! What's happened? What are you doing here?" Paul demanded as he ran up.

"It's Daddy!" Letty informed him.

"He doesn't feel so good," Timmy added solemnly. "His arm hurts."

Uncle Petrie had arrived a second after Paul. "What's the matter with his arm?" he asked quickly.

"He says it's busted," Timmy told him.

"Busted? But how did it get that way?" Uncle Petrie asked.

"He jumped in the ditch," Timmy explained.

Paul didn't wait to hear any more. He hurried into the hospital. But Uncle Petrie asked, "What in the world did he do that for?"

"He didn't want to hurt Pom-Pom," Timmy explained. And Letty burst into tears and hugged the white puppy.

"But how—what was—oh, never mind!" Uncle Petrie said crossly. "It's like pulling teeth to get anything out of some people!" And he turned and stalked off to the hospital after Paul.

Timmy looked after him and sighed. Now, why couldn't Uncle Petrie have let him tell what had happened? Grown-ups certainly acted funny sometimes!

Dr. Wilson came out of the operating room just as Paul joined Meta and Ruth. "There's nothing to worry about, Mrs. Brunson," he explained. "Your husband has a rather bad fracture, but he'll be good as new in a few weeks."

"A few weeks!" She was dismayed and worried.

"As a matter of fact, I may let him come home in a couple of days if you'll promise not to let him try to work!"

But when Dave Brunson came home two days later, he had no desire to go back to plowing and planting. He had decided to give up and take his family back to the city.

He felt bitter about his failure. "I don't know why I ever thought I could run a farm. I was a fool to try," he told Meta, as they sat on the porch late that day.

Meta looked out across the orchard and sighed. A short

time ago she had been the one who didn't want to stay here and try to make a go of farming. Now, when she had found a friend in Ruth Martin and had made plans to join the rest of the Calverton wives and mothers in their various neighborly activities, she had to give them up.

"Can't we stay a little longer?" she asked. "Letty likes it so much here. And people are so kind!" As she spoke, she glanced at the big bouquet of spring flowers that the Ladies' Aiders had brought a few hours before.

"I wish we could," Dave looked glum, "but by the time I can get back to work, it will be too late to do any planting. Summer will be here, and the sun will shrivel the young plants."

Meta was silent, and Dave sighed as he saw her disappointed look.

"Do you suppose we could come back next year—and try again?" she asked timidly. "If you got your old job back in the city—and we saved every cent we could. . . ."

Dave shook his head. "It's no use," he said wearily. "The best thing we can do is to sell the place and go."

"Sell it?" Meta was shocked.

So was Letty, who had started out to the porch with a glass of water for her father. She could hardly believe what she was hearing. She didn't *want* to believe it.

"We have no choice," her father was saying. "After I've paid Dr. Wilson, there won't be enough left in the bank to keep us going more than a month or so."

"Couldn't we ask him to wait till later?"

"Did he ask *me* to wait when I broke this arm? Doctors have to live and pay their own bills!" Dave felt strongly about that.

"I suppose so," Meta sighed. "Will we be leaving soon?"

"I'll put the farm in the hands of the real estate people for immediate sale. I'm sure they'll find a buyer right away." He tried to be cheerful, but it was hard work.

Inside, Letty clapped her hand over her mouth to keep back a cry of protest. Then she set down the glass of water on the hall table and ran to her room.

Once she got there, she climbed up on her bed and let loose a flood of tears into her pillow. She didn't want to go away. She hated the city. She was so happy here. The whole world was against her. She hated everybody. She wouldn't go! She would run away!

There was a faint scratching noise at her closed door and a sad little whimpering.

Letty slid off the bed and ran to open the door. A small

white object flashed past her and leaped up onto the bed. "Oh, Pom-Pom!" She gently put her arms around the puppy. "I know you'll just hate being in the city, same as me." And she started crying all over again, into Pom-Pom's fluffy coat.

But Pom-Pom wriggled away and jumped down off the bed, to run to the window. He stood up on his little hind legs so he could look out, and whined excitedly.

Letty dashed the tears away. "What's the matter?"

"Riff-riff-riff!" Pom-Pom barked, looking down at something in the yard below.

Letty had to look, too. And sure enough, there was a pleasant surprise down there. It was the Martin car, and Timmy and Lassie were just erupting out of it as Mr. and Mrs. Martin walked toward the front porch. "Timmy!" Letty called. "Be down right away!"

Timmy waved and Lassie barked, and then Letty and Pom-Pom raced down the stairs to meet the visitors.

When the greetings were over, Timmy suggested, "Hey, let's go see Taffy. I brought him an apple."

"May we, Mommy, please?" Letty asked eagerly. "He loves apples!"

"All right, dear," Meta nodded.

So Letty and Timmy, and the two dogs, had a race to see who could get to the barn first, and Lassie won. " 'Cause she's got four legs, an' we only have two," Timmy apologized to a breathless Letty.

Pom-Pom brought up the rear. "You'll have to learn to run faster," Letty scolded him. Then she remembered suddenly that they wouldn't be doing any running and racing in the city. "Oh, dear!" Tears filled her eyes.

Timmy didn't even notice them at first. He was giving Taffy the apple, and stroking the long soft nose that the pony had stuck out over the half door of his stall.

When Taffy had crunched the apple into nothing, he nudged Timmy with his nose.

"Look at him beg!" Timmy laughed. Then, "I don't have any more, Taffy. But next time we come, I'll bring you two big fat ones."

"Maybe we won't be here," Letty said tearfully.

"Hey!" Timmy went over to her, scowling. "Whatcha cryin' about?" And when Letty had wailed out the bad news that they were selling the farm and going back to the city, Timmy didn't really believe it. "Aw! You're just makin' that up!" he jeered. But when Letty insisted it was true, Timmy looked almost as woebegone as she did.

"We've got to go away," she said miserably. "Daddy has no money."

"Hey!" Timmy's eyes brightened. "I've got some money! You can have it!"

"Oh, Timmy!" Letty beamed at him. "Really?"

He nodded vigorously, grinning. "It's in my iron bank that belonged to my dad's gran'pa! I can get it out with a knife. You slide the knife in, an' the money comes out on top of the blade. It's easy when you know how!"

"Oh, Timmy!" She was looking admiringly at him. "That'll be wonderful! We won't have to move back to the city! Can I tell Mommy about it? She hates to leave!"

Timmy thought it over, and then shook his head. "Better wait till I bring it over tomorrow, on my bike. You can give it to her for a surprise!"

"Timmy! Letty! Come see what we have!" That was Ruth Martin calling cheerfully from the front steps.

"I bet I know!" Timmy was on his way to the door of the barn. "Come on!" He stopped to call back to Letty, who was giving Taffy a final loving pat and checking to be sure that his blanket hung straight on him and would keep him properly warm all night.

She ran after Timmy, but she stopped in the doorway

and blew a kiss back to the brown pony. "Good night, darling!" she called. "See you tomorrow!" Then she hurried out, with Pom-Pom cavorting at her heels, to follow Timmy and Lassie to the house and the waiting surprise.

It was a big dish of ice cream apiece, and a small dish for each of the dogs. The grownups had theirs, too, but they weren't laughing very much or talking the easy way they usually did. They were hardly even smiling.

Both Timmy and Letty knew that it was the bad news about the Brunsons leaving the farm that was making their parents feel sad. And the youngsters exchanged grins secretly, and had all they could do to keep from giving away their happy plans for a bank robbery!

The Martin family was up early the next morning. Paul had promised Dave Brunson he would go to the real estate office and tell Thad Smith that the farm was up for sale. He hated to do it, but Dave was positive that he was all done with farming. And considering the hard luck he had had, Paul could hardly blame him.

"I wish we could take the place off their hands," Ruth said soberly. "But I guess we have all we can handle here."

"You guess right," Paul agreed. "Money—money—why can't we grow it on trees?"

"If we could, I'd like to plant a money tree in the Brunsons' front yard!" Uncle Petrie said wryly. "Sure hate to see them move away again. Why can't that Brunson boy have the know-how his pa did?"

"Don't forget he left before he had a chance to get it! You don't inherit that," Paul reminded him. "You learn it!"

There was an Indian war whoop from the front yard.

"Sounds like you've got company!" Paul told Timmy.

But Timmy frowned. Why did Boomer have to come just when *he* had something mighty important to 'tend to?

"Hey, Timmy!" Boomer knocked on the screen door and came in, all at once. "Pa says it's okay to go anywhere we want to, now. The burglar's gone."

"I know," Timmy said soberly. He went on eating.

"Well, come on, then!" Boomer was puzzled by Timmy's lack of interest. "Let's go fishing!"

"Don't feel like it. *You* go!" Timmy scraped the bottom of his bowl, though it was quite empty. "I'm busy eating."

"Why, Timmy!" His mother gasped at such rudeness.

"Okay, okay!" Boomer glared at Timmy. "If you'd rather be a sissy an' play with that silly girl an' her silly pup, it's okay with me. Go ahead!" He turned on his heel and marched noisily to the door and down the steps.

"Timmy!" Paul said sternly. "I think you'd better go apologize to Boomer."

"I didn't say anything!" Timmy scowled back at him. *"He* said it!"

"I believe you'd better go to your room and think it over," Paul said, gesturing toward the hallway.

"Yes, sir!" Timmy got off his chair and marched to the hall door and out of sight down the hall.

They heard the bedroom door close after him, before Uncle Petrie let himself chuckle out loud. "Spunky little rascal!" he said, grinning. "Didn't want company, and he just said so! Too bad grownups can't be that honest!"

"There's no excuse for rudeness," Ruth reminded him briskly. She watched Boomer ride away on his bike. Then she sighed, "And I was planning to take Timmy to town with us and buy him a new suit! Now what do I do?"

"Let him stay where he is and think over his sins," Paul grinned a little. "If you weaken and take him to town now, he'll be sure he won the decision!"

"Oh, dear!" Ruth sighed. "He'll hate being left home."

But that was one time that Ruth was wrong about Timmy. Being left home suited him perfectly on this particular morning.

16

TIMMY TRIES TO HELP

Timmy stood at the window, watching his family out in the yard. First it was his dad who left, in the pickup truck. Lassie was down there, frolicking around as if she hoped that she and Timmy were going to be invited along. When Paul drove off without saying anything like "Go get Timmy" to her, she stood looking after the truck, and her tail-wagging slowed down till finally it stopped altogether. Then she turned and went over to the garage, where Ruth was backing the sedan out.

It looked to Timmy, when Ruth also drove off without inviting him and Lassie to go along, as if he were going to be left quite alone. But for once, he didn't mind it. He had something to do that was very important.

He waited till Uncle Petrie had disappeared into the barn and was busy there, whistling at his work. Then he hurried to the kitchen to get a broad-bladed knife.

Lassie heard him rattling things in the knife drawer, and she pushed open the screen door to join him.

Timmy wasn't supposed to touch the knives, but he felt that it wouldn't be wrong to disobey for just this once, seeing that it wasn't any kind of a cutting job he was planning to do.

Back in his room, and with Lassie watching him with a great deal of interest, he sat on the floor with his old iron bank. It was shaped like a house, and it said FIRST NATIONAL BANK on the front. There was a slit in the side where the coins were dropped in.

Very carefully, Timmy inserted the blade of the knife in the coin slit, shook the bank, and turned it sideways so the coins could come sliding out on the knife blade. But only one came out, a penny.

He tried again, impatiently. This time, not even a penny slid out. The coins had piled up across the opening. And even though he shook and shook, he couldn't seem to get one to slide out on the knife.

After a few minutes more of shaking and probing, all he had were two more pennies. It was very discouraging. At that rate, it would take him all day to get a quarter's worth!

He dropped the three pennies back into the bank, and told Lassie sadly, "Guess we'll have to think of some other way to get the money for Letty's folks."

But Lassie was no help at all. She was more interested in trying to coax him to come outside and play.

"You don't understand," he told her crossly, "we *have* to get them a lot of money, or they'll move away."

He glanced around the room, without much hope of getting an idea. Suddenly he caught his breath and scrambled to his feet. There was something on the very top shelf of his toy closet that might be the answer.

He hurried over and opened the closet door. It was there, all right. His most precious belonging. It was the scale model of the fighter plane that his father had piloted during the Korean war. Paul had spent many evenings building it for Timmy.

Timmy pulled over the step stool and climbed up so he could lift the plane down carefully. There was a little dust on it, but that didn't matter. His dad had told him some exciting stories about the big plane whose model this was. He particularly remembered now that he had said, "They cost nearly a million dollars apiece, these fighters!" Well, if the big ones cost a million dollars, he decided, one this size ought to be worth a lot of money, too. And maybe he could find somebody who would like to buy it. He didn't want to part with it, but he had nothing else he could sell.

Uncle Petrie was still busy when Timmy came out of the kitchen door carrying a towel-wrapped object, and rode his bike off hastily toward town, with Lassie running at his heels.

Sam Moss was surprised to see Timmy come into the grocery store a little later, carrying something wrapped in a towel. "Be with you in a minute, Timmy," he called to the youngster, and finished waiting on a customer. He had waited on Ruth Martin a while ago, and felt sure that Timmy had wheedled an extra nickel for candy out of her.

When the customer left, Sam went behind the candy counter and leaned over. "Which will it be today, son? Got some licorice shoelaces, penny apiece!"

Timmy shook his head and tried not to look at the tempting display. "I don't want to buy anything. I got somethin' to sell you."

"Sell me?" Sam grinned. He guessed that Timmy might have some half-wilted wild flowers in that towel-wrapped bundle, or some walnuts he had found among last autumn's fallen leaves. But Timmy carefully unwrapped his plane.

Sam Moss was surprised, and a little shocked. He had sold Paul Martin some of the parts for that small plane, and Paul had told him later how Timmy prized it. "He wouldn't part with it for anything in the world!" Paul had said. "I do believe he loves it almost as much as he loves Lassie!"

Yet here was the boy offering it for sale!

"How much will you give me for it?" Timmy asked seriously.

"Well, now—I'll have to think that over," Sam pulled his ear and cocked his head to one side, for all the world like Lassie when she was thinking. "What would you say to—uh—fifty thousand?" His eyes twinkled.

Timmy frowned. "Is that a lot of money? 'Cause I've got to have a *big* lot."

Sam chuckled. "A man with that much would be real rich!"

Timmy's eyes brightened. "You mean he wouldn't have to give up the farm and go away someplace else?"

"Give up—the farm?" Sam Moss looked startled. "Why, no. I guess he wouldn't, all right."

Now he was wishing he hadn't tried to joke about it. He had no idea that the Martins were in such a desperate condition! Ruth Martin had made only a few purchases, he remembered suddenly. And she hadn't bought that suit for Timmy that she had talked about last week. So maybe they *were* in a bad way for money.

"Okay, then," Timmy nodded gravely, "I'll take it." He was being very brave, but in spite of himself he had to stroke the shiny painted side of the fighter plane in farewell.

"To tell the truth, Timmy," Sam Moss said apologetically, "I haven't that much in the register right now. But how would five silver dollars do till I can get the rest?"

"Well," Timmy knitted his forehead, "I guess it'll be all right. That's a whole lot of money, too, isn't it?"

"Some people would say it's a spanking good sum," Sam agreed. Then he went to the register and hit the key hard, and the bell rang and the drawer popped out.

He brought the five silver dollars around the corner of the counter, and put them into Timmy's shirt pocket. "There you are, son," he said, smiling. "Now, wait a second." He took a safety pin out of his apron, and pinned the pocket shut. "Now they won't fall out on the way home!"

"Thank you, Mr. Moss," Timmy said soberly. "Come on, Lassie. We gotta hurry now." And he started toward the door.

But before he went out, he had to turn for a last look at the precious plane model. Then he scooted down the steps to his bike and rode off, a bit wobbly, with Lassie running beside him.

Sam Moss looked at the dusty little plane on the counter, and gently drew the ends of the towel around it. Then he put it out of sight under the counter, and went to wait on the customer who had just come in. But he wasn't through with the situation. There were some things he intended to say to Paul Martin tonight, on the phone, about being so stiff-necked that he wouldn't come to his friends for help in time of need!

It took Timmy and Lassie over an hour to get to the old Forbidden Valley farm. The hill would have been shorter, but Timmy never took his bicycle up a steep place like that, so he had to go around on the valley road.

He found Letty riding her pony near the gate. She had

been waiting for him since early morning.

"Did you get the money?" she asked eagerly, even before he had a chance to get off his bike.

"Sure did!" Timmy grinned, patting his pocket and making the silver dollars clink. "Just wait till I show you!"

Letty was off the pony in a flash, and ran to examine the bright silver dollars that Timmy proudly displayed. Neither of them had ever seen such a lot of money before. It looked like a fortune.

"Was it hard gettin' 'em out of your bank?" Letty asked, her eyes round.

Timmy shook his head. "Didn't get 'em out of my bank," he said, and told her the whole story.

"You mean—you sold your plane?" Letty gasped unbelievingly when he had finished. "Oh, Timmy . . . ." She was silent for a minute, staring at him. But her distress was short-lived.

"Now we won't have to move back to the city!" she exclaimed, unable to conceal her delight. "Oh, thank you, Timmy! You're wonderful!"

And when Timmy made her hold out her apron so he could drop the jingling dollars into it, she danced up and down excitedly, while Pom-Pom ran in circles, yipping happily, and Lassie added her own bark to the racket.

"Better give it to your mom before you lose some of it!" Timmy advised through the din.

"Oh, I will! I will right now!" Letty agreed, and she didn't even wait to get back on her pony, but ran down the road toward the house, with the silver dollars clinking in her apron. "See you later!" floated back to Timmy.

"Well," Timmy told Lassie, "I guess we better go home." In spite of himself, he couldn't help feeling disappointed. Somewhere in the back of his mind, he had been hoping that a miracle might have happened between last night and now, and that the Brunsons wouldn't need any money after all. He would have been able to take the silver dollars back to Mr. Moss and ask for his plane. But now it was gone forever.

He pedaled slowly back to the road that led off to his own home, and not even Lassie's frolicsome pursuit of a saucy chipmunk that challenged her from a fallen log could cheer him up.

And when he got home, he found trouble waiting for him.

Ruth Martin had been waiting for a couple of hours for her son to come home. There was a stormy look in her eyes as she sat in the living room and glanced from time to time at the mantel clock.

She had gone straight to Timmy's room when she had come home. She hadn't really expected him to be there. Nothing had been said about his having to stay there all day. That would have been too severe a punishment for his rudeness to Boomer.

When she had opened the door and looked in, the first thing that met her eye had been the bank, lying on its side on the floor. Then she had seen the shiny-bladed knife near it, and she hadn't had to guess very hard what it meant. Timmy had robbed his bank!

She had picked up the bank and noticed that it still seemed pretty heavy. At least, he hadn't emptied it!

But the knife! The sharpest one in the kitchen, the one she herself hardly dared use for fear it would slip and slice off a finger. And he had brazenly taken it—in spite of orders—and then had left it lying here dangerously.

Ruth had made up her mind that this time there would be no coddling. Timmy had earned a severe punishment. And she wasn't going to be smiled or coaxed out of it.

She had had no reason to look into Timmy's toy closet, so she didn't even suspect that his model plane was no

longer in its place of honor on the shelf.

Uncle Petrie came into the room as she sat rocking in the old fashioned cane-bottomed rocker. He had already heard about Timmy's offense. "Ruthie," he began uneasily, "don't be too hard on him. Maybe he remembered somebody's birthday all of a sudden, and had to have money for a present."

Ruth spoke coldly. "He could have waited and asked for it. And there's no excuse for taking that knife."

Uncle Petrie tried to joke. "Well, there's no blood around, so I guess he didn't have any accident."

"Uncle Petrie," Ruth snapped, "that isn't funny!"

Uncle Petrie sighed. "I know, Ruthie. Guess I'll go get washed up." And he went into his own room and closed the door.

Ruth heard a light step in the kitchen. "Timmy!" she called sternly, "come in here!"

"Yes'm!" he answered cheerfully, and when he came in with Lassie at his heels, he was surprised to see Ruth's frown.

She gestured toward the center table. His bank and the knife were lying there. "Why did you take money out of your bank?" she asked abruptly.

"But I didn't!" Timmy was surprised at the tone of her voice.

"Timmy! Don't make it worse by fibbing! I found your bank on the floor in your room and that horrible big kitchen knife beside it!"

"But—" Timmy was bewildered, "I'm not tellin' a fib, Mom. Honest!"

"I suppose you didn't disobey me and take that knife out of the kitchen drawer so you could get into your bank!" Ruth accused him.

"I—guess I did—but—" Timmy started, but Ruth interrupted him.

"You'd better go to your room. And this time, you'd better stay there. I'm going to talk to your father about this the moment he comes home. I'm afraid he's going to have to find some way to teach you not to tell fibs. I can't stand people who lie, and neither can he."

Timmy stared at her helplessly a second, then he turned and stumbled toward the hall door, head hanging. Lassie went with him, and Ruth heard them go into the bedroom and close the door.

She was still angry with him. What was wrong with him that he would try to fib, even though she had found the bank and the knife on his floor?

And when Paul came home a little later, she was almost in tears as she told him about it.

He frowned as she finished. "It isn't like Timmy to lie. Did he tell you why he wanted to rob his own bank?"

She shook her head and sighed. "He wouldn't even admit that he had done it!"

"Maybe going without supper tonight will teach him a lesson about lying!" Paul said grimly.

There was a flash of lights across the windows of the living room and the sound of an old motor as a car pulled into the farmyard.

"Company!" Ruth said, but without any enthusiasm. She didn't feel like entertaining anyone.

17

BAD NEWS

Paul went toward the front door to see who their unexpected visitor was, but he stopped as the telephone bell rang sharply in their signal.

"I'll get it," Ruth told him and hurried to answer the ring. "Why, hello, Mr. Moss . . . of course . . . I'll call him right away." She beckoned to Paul and as he came to the phone she told him quickly, "He sounds upset. I'll go see who's outside."

She was surprised to see the Brunson car. Meta was just getting out of it. "Why, Meta! How nice to see you! How is Dave?"

"He's doing very well, thanks," Meta told her, "but he

wanted me to come right over and bring this to you." She had something in the hand she held out, and Ruth held out her own hand for it, surprised.

Ruth was still more surprised when she discovered that the heavy object that Meta dropped into her palm was a small stack of silver dollars. "Why, what on earth . . . ?"

"It was the most touching thing I've ever heard of. I cried when Letty told me what Timmy had done, the darling," Meta told his bewildered mother.

"I don't understand," Ruth said. "What *did* Timmy do? And why are you giving me this money?"

"I thought sure he must have told you!" It was Meta's turn to be surprised. Then she told Ruth about Timmy's generous sacrifice of his most prized possession, the model plane, so Letty and her family could stay on the farm.

There were tears in Ruth's own eyes when Meta Brunson finished. "Poor little fellow! We had no idea."

"Please tell him we appreciated it, anyhow, even if we can't take it," Meta told her.

"I wish there were some way you could stay on at the farm," Ruth said sadly.

Meta shook her head and smiled bravely. "There isn't."

Meanwhile, Paul had gotten a surprise from Sam Moss.

"I thought we were friends!" Sam had barked over the phone at him.

"Why, what's wrong, Sam? Of course we're friends!" Paul answered.

"Then why didn't you come to me when you needed money?"

"Money? I don't know what you're talking about, Sam," Paul assured him.

"I'm talking about you needing money so bad that you've got to give up the farm—and not coming to me, your friend, for help!" He stopped shouting and added, in a reproachful voice, "That hurts me, Paul. It hurts me."

"But I'm *not* giving up the farm! And I'm not broke—not any more than usual, that is! Good heavens, where did you get that idea?" He laughed heartily.

There was a shocked silence at the other end of the line for a moment, then Sam said evenly, "If you ain't broke, why did you let the kid sell his plane? What's going on?"

When the stunned father had found his voice, he asked Sam Moss to give him the whole story from the beginning.

As he hung up the receiver at last, after assuring Sam Moss that it was really someone else who needed the money, and not the Martin family, he turned to see Ruth standing in the doorway. She was looking at him with a strange expression on her face and holding out something in her fist.

"That was Meta Brunson out there, and she brought me this." She opened her hand to show him the five shiny silver dollars. "It seems he didn't rob his bank, after all. I misjudged him."

"We both did," he told her solemnly. "I think I'll go talk to the little fellow."

"I have some apologizing to do, myself," Ruth admitted.

They started toward his room together, but as they went down the hallway arm in arm, she stopped suddenly. "He still disobeyed orders about handling the knife," she reminded Paul in a low voice. "He should be punished for that."

"Could we sort of forget it, just this once?" Paul asked with an appealing grin.

"But he might have cut himself badly!" she answered, sternly. "Next time—"

Paul interrupted. "There won't be any next time. I'll give him a good talking to—later. But not tonight. Huh?"

Ruth threw up her hands. "You men certainly stick together!" she told him, but there was a twinkle in her eye as she took his arm again and they went on into Timmy's room.

Neither of them knew exactly what to say as they faced their small son. But Timmy saved them the decision. He came to the point at once, before they had time to speak.

"I'm sorry I took the knife. I won't ever do it again. But I *didn't* take the money out of my bank, honest!" he told them soberly.

Paul put his arm around Timmy's shoulder and sat beside him on the edge of the bed. "We know, skipper," he assured Timmy. "And we know all about selling the model to get money for the Brunsons."

"Now they don't have to go away, do they?" Timmy asked eagerly.

"Mr. Brunson thinks it would be better if they did, anyhow, son. He thinks it was very fine of you to get them the money the way you did, but there are a lot of other things that make it a good idea for them to go back to the city to live."

Timmy looked puzzled and worried. "But Letty doesn't want to go! Where will she keep her pony if they live in the city?"

"That's up to them, skipper," Paul told him gravely.

"And in the meantime, we're going to town tomorrow to buy back your plane for you."

Timmy felt very sorry to think that the Brunsons had to go away, but he was happy about getting his plane back.

And the next morning he went to Calverton with his dad and saw the five silver dollars go back into Sam Moss's cash register in exchange for his model plane.

Black clouds were gathering in the north, and the wind had gone down to a whisper of warm breath, by the time Timmy and his father were on their way home.

Timmy carried the model carefully into the house, still wrapped in the towel. He went to his room at once and put the plane back on the upper shelf of the toy cabinet. Then he stood staring at it for a moment, admiringly, before he closed and latched the cabinet door.

Lassie had followed him in, and she stood watching him. When the cabinet was closed, she said, "Wroof!" and backed invitingly toward the door. She seemed to be saying, "Well, that's that. Now let's go and play!"

But Timmy didn't feel like playing. He was thinking about the Brunsons having to leave the valley, and remembering how happy Letty had been when she thought they could stay on.

Ruth was busy in the kitchen, stirring something in a pot on the stove. Uncle Petrie was finishing his lunch. And out in the yard Paul had the tires off the sedan, changing them around so they would wear more evenly.

"This chicken stew is almost done, but from the looks of the car out there, I'm afraid I won't get it out to Dave Brunson for hours," Ruth told Uncle Petrie.

"I s'pose I could take it over in the pickup," Uncle Petrie offered reluctantly, "but I was countin' on layin' a coat of paint on that shed this afternoon."

"Mom! Can I take it on my bike? It'd ride just fine in my wire basket!" Timmy offered.

"I don't see why not!" Ruth agreed. "But don't stay too long. The radio says that storm is almost here!"

"I'll be back in a hurry," Timmy promised, "long before it starts raining!"

But some big drops the size of pennies had started falling even before Timmy got to the Brunsons' valley with Lassie beside him and the stew riding safely in the covered pot in the wire basket.

Meta was delighted with the thoughtful offering, and Dave's gloomy face lighted up at the sight of the tasty food. "They're fine people, the Martins," he said quietly. "We would have gotten to be good friends, I know."

"Dave," Meta asked, "couldn't we—*mortgage* the place, and stay on?"

He shook his head sadly. "Paul thought of that, and he talked to the bankers yesterday. They reminded him that without a crop, I'd have no way of meeting payments." He made a wry grimace. "So—they had to turn us down." His hand was on hers. "I don't want to leave here either, dear. But we have no other choice."

Timmy knew, as the raindrops began coming down more heavily, that he and Lassie really should be starting for home. But he had to go look for Letty and spend a few minutes petting Taffy before he left.

He and Lassie found Letty trying to convince Pom-Pom that he shouldn't be afraid of falling off Taffy's back. But every time that Letty lifted him into Taffy's saddle and told him to stay there, the white puppy jumped right down again, and ran into a dark corner of the barn to hide.

"I guess I'll never get him trained like the poodles in the circus," she confided to Timmy after they had all said hello to each other.

"Maybe if Lassie showed him how, he wouldn't be scared," Timmy suggested.

But that was one time that Lassie refused firmly to take orders. She backed away in spite of all Timmy's coaxing and stern commands, and ran over to hide in the same dark corner where Pom-Pom had taken refuge.

That made Letty giggle, but the giggle stopped suddenly as they heard a big vehicle come creaking into the yard and stop outside the barn. "Wonder who that is."

Timmy and she both went to look out into the rain-filled yard.

"Oh, it's the man who sold Taffy to us!" she exclaimed.

It was a big van, and on the side of it, large letters proclaimed that it belonged to the Elite Dog and Pony Show. It was painted red, white and blue, in all sorts of curlicues and patterns, with a fine gilt trim, sort of gingerbready and fancy.

"Maybe he's got another pony to sell!" Timmy's eyes sparkled with excitement. "Maybe my folks would buy it!"

"Guess I'll go find out!" Letty announced. "And if he has a cute one, I'll ask Daddy to tell *your* dad you'd like to have it!"

"Yeah! I guess that's better than *me* askin'," Timmy decided. "But I sure would like to know." He looked longingly at the wagon, from which they could hear various thumpings that seemed to indicate that there were ponies inside.

The rain was really coming down now, and there was a big clap of thunder that seemed to come from right over-head.

"Golly! I guess I better get on home right away!" Timmy decided hastily. "I'll come over tomorrow and find out what happened!"

Letty pulled off her apron and threw it over her head like a shawl. Then she picked up Pom-Pom and cuddled him under it with her. "Okay! See you tomorrow!" she told Timmy and dashed for the house.

Timmy turned up his collar, whistled Lassie to him, and ran for his bike. A moment later, he was headed up the lane, homeward bound.

Letty came into the kitchen, a little wet from the short run in the heavy rain. There was a brisk little fire in the old stove, and she set Pom-Pom down in front of it while she got an old towel to dry off his soft white coat.

The door to the living room was open, and Letty could hear the voices of her father and mother and the pony man. At first, she didn't pay much attention, but suddenly something the man said made her stop and listen.

"I can take the pony tomorrow," the man was saying in his harsh, loud voice. "I can't wait any longer than that, because I'm booked for Capitol City Fair Grounds this weekend and I won't be back this way."

"Couldn't you leave him here just a few days more? I'd like some time to explain to our little girl that we can't take him to the city with us!" It was her mother's voice.

"Lady, it's tomorrow or nothin'!" the harsh voice said. "I'm giving you more than the critter's worth, as it is. I sold him to you in the first place because I couldn't teach him any tricks. I'm doin' you a favor buying him back."

"What time tomorrow?" That was her father speaking. His voice sounded tired.

"Early. I wanta be on the road by eight or eight thirty."

"All right. He'll be in the barn, waiting."

"I'll bring the cash with me," the man said, and Letty heard the scrape of a chair on the bare floor.

She snatched up Pom-Pom, bundled him in the old towel, and ran to the door into the hall. She closed it softly behind her as the pony show man came into the kitchen with Meta Brunson.

"I'll give you a fair price for any tack you've bought for him, saddle and whatnot. You won't be needing it any more," the man told Meta. Then, in a kinder voice, he added, "Too bad things didn't work out, ma'am."

Meta looked surprised. "Why, thank you!" she said, "that's very kind of you."

And when the gruff-spoken showman had driven the big van out of the yard through the pouring rain, she went back to Dave, in the living room, and told him, "People *are* friendlier in the country, aren't they? Oh, I wish we could stay!"

"So do I, dear," Dave told her softly. "So do I." But there was no hope in his voice, only resignation.

"I think I'd better go tell Letty about the pony now," Meta said. It wasn't going to be easy to do, she thought, but she had to be told.

Letty was in her own room, looking out at the driving rain, with Pom-Pom on her lap. She took the news about Taffy very calmly, much to her mother's relief.

"I guess he *would* be a nuisance in the city," Letty agreed soberly, after Meta had made a full explanation.

Meta put her arms around Letty affectionately. "Darling, I'm so glad you understand. We'd never sell Taffy if there were only some way we could keep him."

"I know, Mommy," Letty nodded. She patted her mother

on the shoulder. "It's not your fault." And Meta, with her own eyes brimming, couldn't see a trace of tears in Letty's.

She went back to Dave with a lighter heart, to tell him how bravely Letty had taken the bad news. "She didn't even cry. And I know how much that pony means to her!"

But if Letty hadn't cried then, she made up for it during the long night, before the first streaks of dawn showed in the rain-swept sky.

All night the rain had kept up without slackening, and it was still coming down now in a steady downpour that threatened to flood the lowlands and overflow the creeks.

Invalided Dave Brunson and his wife slept soundly in the gray dawn. But Letty moved hastily about her room, getting dressed for a last ride. She had made up her mind to it during the long night.

Quietly, she let herself out of the house and ran to the barn. But quiet as she was, someone else had watched her every move. And as she hurriedly saddled up Taffy, Pom-Pom waited close at hand to go along with them, and Letty couldn't make him go back to the house.

When she was ready to leave, she picked up the white puppy and dropped him into the empty stall and closed the half door on him. "I'll be back, Pom-Pom darling."

18

THE RUNAWAY

It was starting to rain again, but gently now, as Letty rode her pony down the road in the direction of Timmy Martin's house. She was sorry that she had had to lock up poor little Pom-Pom, but she planned to be back again in a couple of hours to let him out.

The ride seemed to be endless, in the gray early morning, but finally she came in sight of the Martins' white fence, and then soon she was in the farmyard. And she had only been riding less than an hour.

She rode toward the barn, expecting that Timmy would come charging out at any moment to meet her. But even Lassie wasn't anywhere to be seen.

Timmy was still fast asleep in his room, and Ruth was the only Martin awake so far, on this rainy morning.

Lassie, lying on her blanket beside Timmy's bed, lifted her head and listened. Then she padded over to the open window, pushed aside the curtain with her nose, and stared out. A moment later, she had leaped through the window and was running across the farmyard to greet the tired, wet little girl who was dismounting from her pony.

Her bark of greeting was loud and cheerful, and it brought Timmy stumbling out of bed and to the window, to see what Lassie had found to bark at so early in the morning. One look, and he was wide awake and rushing to get his clothes on.

Two minutes later he was out of the house, fully dressed except for one shoe, which he just couldn't wait to put on before he went to say hello. "Hey! What are you doing here?" he demanded, waving the shoe at her.

"I brought Taffy for you," she told him.

"For *me?*" Timmy was astonished.

She nodded solemnly. "We have to sell him. So I thought maybe your folks would buy him for you." She was trying hard to be brave, but her voice broke in spite of herself. "That pony man wants to take him away this morning, so I had to bring him over early."

"Golly, I'd sure like to own him!" Timmy stroked the pony's soft brown nose.

"If you buy him, maybe I can come see him sometimes," Letty said, laying her cheek against the pony's neck.

Ruth Martin leaned out of the kitchen window. "Letty! Where did you come from at this hour of the morning? How about some breakfast with us?"

Letty was glad to be inside the warm, pleasant kitchen and out of the rain. But she didn't care about any breakfast, right away. She wouldn't be hungry till she knew that Taffy was going to be safe with Timmy and his folks.

Paul Martin came in as she was explaining her errand, and he looked very serious about it. "I'm sorry, honey," he told her, "but your daddy has already agreed to sell Taffy to the pony man. That makes it a promise, and the pony man is probably counting on using Taffy for his act. You can't ask your dad to go back on his promise. It wouldn't be fair to the pony man."

"But I don't want him to have Taffy!" she protested. "He'll take him away where I'll never see him any more!"

"He has a right to, once he's made a deal to buy him," Ruth explained gently. "Can't you see that?"

"I s'pose so," she admitted tearfully. "But he doesn't like Taffy. He doesn't think he's smart. Maybe he'll even b-beat him when Taffy can't learn tricks! Oh, please take him! He'll be so happy here!"

"I'm sorry, Letty," Timmy's father told her, "but you'd better take him back home now. The pony man will be looking for him."

Letty saw from their faces that it was no use. She picked up her raincoat and started hastily toward the door.

"Wait, dear. You're not going without some warm food inside you," Ruth told her firmly, "and then Uncle Petrie can drive you home in the pickup, and Taffy can trot along behind it."

Letty backed toward the door. "I have to see how Taffy is, first. I'll—I'll be back!" She turned suddenly and flew out the door into the rain.

Lassie ran to the door and looked after her, barking.

"She's comin' back, Lassie," Timmy assured the collie. "Whatcha fussin' for?"

But Lassie kept on barking, and when Timmy ran to the door to look out, he was just in time to see Letty riding out of the yard at a fast trot. "Mom! She's riding away!" he shouted.

"Oh, dear!" Ruth was just a little annoyed at the stubborn child. "At least she could have let us take her home!"

But Letty wasn't going home. When she had gone a mile or so on the dirt road, she cut off suddenly into the woods.

The rain was coming down steadily now, and the flash of distant lightning promised even more storm.

She rode along the narrow woods path, so familiar now to her. Taffy was a little skittish when the thunder rolled, off in the distance, but she patted his neck and told him soothingly, "Don't be scared. It's only thunder."

When she came to the creek, she noticed that there was a lot more water in it than usual, and the water was racing along at great speed. She didn't notice that there was a place just ahead where the water had cut into the bank.

Taffy stumbled, struggled to regain his footing, and neighed in terror as he felt the soft bank giving 'way under his feet and throwing him off balance.

Letty sawed at the reins, trying to pull him back to safety, but she herself slipped in the saddle, her foot came out of the stirrup and she fell and rolled halfway down the bank.

If she hadn't been wet enough before, she certainly was now, as she scrambled back up the bank with the rain lashing against her face.

Through the heavy brush, she could just make out a glimpse of the brown pony, and then he disappeared. She ran as fast as she could, through the tangle of bushes and saplings, calling "Taffy! Come back!" But she didn't get another sight of him.

When she finally stopped, bramble torn, soaking, and tearful, she was lost.

The woods were dark here. She had never been this deep in the tangled brush. And the murky sky overhead made the place spooky and frightening.

"Taffy!" she called. But she knew he wouldn't come.

She sat down on a rock and cried, and her tears mingled with the rain until, suddenly, a most welcome shaft of sunlight beamed down and spread over the rock. The warmth of it stopped the chattering of her teeth, but she huddled there forlornly, too frightened to try to find her way back to the creek and the familiar path along the top of the bank. She had dropped her riding glove somewhere, but she didn't bother to look for it, in her terrified misery.

The pony man was driving his big van into the farmyard when Meta came to the kitchen door to see who it was so early in the morning. She had half forgotten that he had said he would be there first thing in the morning.

"Oh, dear! He *is* early!" she told Dave, frowning. "Do you think we should wake up Letty so she can say good-by to Taffy?"

Dave Brunson, in his pajamas and with his broken arm in a sling, shook his head. "Better not. If Taffy's gone when she gets up, it might be easier on her."

She agreed soberly. Then Dave slipped a raincoat over his shoulders and went out to meet the pony man and to deliver Taffy and the harness to him in exchange for the money.

Meta tiptoed up to Letty's room and softly pushed the door open. If Letty was awake, she would need her mother's arms to comfort her over the loss of her pet.

But Letty wasn't there!

Meta thought she knew where to find her. She went slowly downstairs and out to the barn. But there was no sign of her there, either. And Taffy's stall was empty except for Pom-Pom, who barked indignantly at them and rushed out to jump all over them when they opened the half door.

The pony man was angry. "What kind of a deal is this? Where's the pony?"

"We don't know any more about it than you do," Dave

Brunson said sharply. "The child has probably taken him for a last ride. She'll be back soon."

"Well, I don't have time to wait for her," the scowling showman told them. "I'm calling off the deal. I didn't want him much anyhow. I was just trying to do you folks a favor by taking him off your hands."

Dave and Meta watched him drive the big pony van out of the yard, and for a moment neither of them spoke. Then Dave smiled crookedly. "I'm sort of glad it didn't work out, after all. We'll find somebody to buy him, I'm sure!"

Meta nodded, smiling back at him. Then she sobered. "It's naughty of her to act like this. You'll have to scold her for it."

"Me?" Dave grinned. "It's up to you. She's yours, too!"

"Dave Brunson, you never want to—" Meta was shaking her finger at him playfully, but she glanced past him at something that had caught her eye far down the road behind him, and her face went white. "Dave! Look!"

He wheeled and stared, and his own face turned the color of putty. Taffy was trotting toward them. He looked very perky and proud of himself, with his mane and tail flowing in the breeze, but he was caked with mud halfway up his legs, and the saddle was hanging 'way over to one side.

The reins were dragging on the ground.

"Something's happened to my baby!" Meta cried out, and for a moment it looked as if she might be going to fall in a faint. Dave caught her with his well arm, and held her.

"Meta!" He spoke loudly to make her stop her hysterical sobbing. "Stop that! Maybe she dismounted and Taffy ran away! You know what a tricky fellow he is!"

"But—the twisted saddle! I know she's lying in the road somewhere, badly hurt!"

"You don't know anything of the sort," he insisted. He was stilling his own fears while he tried to calm hers.

"I'm going to find her!" she announced, trying to wrench free and run up the road. But Dave held her firmly.

"Wait, dear! We don't know what direction Taffy came from. We can't just rush blindly around, and miss her. The best thing for us to do is to get the car out and we'll try to trace Taffy's hoofprints back along the road. Maybe we'll meet her coming along on foot!"

"Oh, I hope so!" Meta rushed to the house to get the car keys and start the search.

But when she came out with the keys, Paul Martin and Uncle Petrie were driving up in their truck. She ran to them.

"Letty's missing!" she called excitedly.

Uncle Petrie spoke under his breath to Paul. "Doggone! You were right, Paul. You figured she'd run off with that cussed pony rather'n give him up!"

Paul nodded with a grave expression. "Don't worry, Meta," he told the young mother. "We'll find her fast." He jumped out of the truck and told Uncle Petrie, "Get Carl and a couple of his boys. We'll do this right." He had noticed the twisted saddle right away, and was afraid that Meta's fears of Letty having been hurt were going to be realized.

"I'm going along!" Meta announced, but Paul caught Dave's eye and shook his head warningly.

Dave understood. He put his arm around Meta's waist and told her quietly, "You'd only be in the way, dear. Better wait right here till they bring her back!"

"That's right, ma'am," Uncle Petrie leaned out of the truck and managed to give her a reassuring grin. "The young'un will be needing a good hot bath to get the mud off, judgin' by Taffy's looks!"

"I'll light the water heater and lay out some clean clothes." Meta seemed convinced by Uncle Petrie's cheerfulness that everything was going to be all right.

A few minutes later, Uncle Petrie had roared off down

the road to get the sheriff and a couple of his deputies, and Paul and Dave were setting out to backtrack the pony to find out where he had come from.

The pony's trail—clear in the damp, sandy road—came from the woods. But once they had followed it that far, it was lost in the damp fallen leaves. They were stopped.

Paul Martin cupped his hands around his mouth and called "Letty! Letty!" turning from one direction to the other. But there was no answer.

It wouldn't be easy finding her, wherever she was.

Deep in the tangled brush, beyond a series of low hills, Letty was still sitting on the sunny rock. She felt warm now and more hopeful of finding her way home again. She was pretty sure that Taffy would head straight for the barn, the bad little fellow! And she wondered if the pony show man would still be waiting to take Taffy away with him. She guessed he would be.

She sniffled a little and a tear coursed down through the mud on her cheek. Darling Taffy!

She heard something crashing through the brush in her direction, and she jumped up and stared around her in fright. It sounded awfully big—like a bear, perhaps!

Now she located the direction of the smashing, crashing

noise. It was off to one side, but she couldn't see anything yet. Maybe there was still time to hide.

She picked up a stick—a very small stick, as it happened, but it made her feel a little safer, anyhow. Then, stick in hand, she darted behind a boulder and crouched as close under a thick green bush as she could get.

She hardly dared to look out, as the noise came closer, but she ventured one tiny peek.

Now the brush crasher had come into sight. It was a big man with a bristling black beard and the biggest feet she thought she had ever seen! He had two dead rabbits slung over his shoulder, and there was a revolver in his belt.

She held her breath and shrank closer to the boulder. But the man stalked on past her—hardly two yards away— and crashed his way into the darkness of the woods.

For a moment, she was tempted to call out and run after him. She thought he might be able to tell her which way to go to get safely out of the woods again.

But something had held her back. Perhaps it was the bushy black beard, or the small animal-like eyes. More probably, it was the sight of those poor little rabbits!

Whatever it was, she didn't call to him. And it was just as well that she hadn't!

19

LASSIE HELPS OUT

The black-bearded man who called himself Blondy, to confuse old Joey, was getting ready to pull out. The heavy rain had made the cave damp and miserable, and old Joey had been more than ever wrapped in his own silence.

Joey watched the big man toss the dead rabbits on the ground near the fire, but he made no move to start to skin them and get them ready for the stew that Blondy wanted.

"What's eating you now?" the black-bearded one snarled. "Hurry up! I'm getting hungry."

Joey eyed the rabbits gloomily and shook his head. "Ain't going to touch them. That little feller with the dark splotch on his shoulder was a particular friend of mine. Fed

255

right out of my hand. You can cook him yourself."

"Why, you crazy old galoot! I oughta—" The big man glared at Joey, and his hand hovered over the butt of his revolver. Then, suddenly, he laughed and relaxed. "Okay. I'll cook your pal. And I'll make a good meal for myself. And what's left, I'll take along with me."

"Where you going?" Old Joey's eyes brightened.

"Far away as I can get, old man. I'll be as batty as you are, if I stick around much longer!"

"You aren't figuring to turn me in to the law, are you?" Joey asked fearfully.

"Not a chance!" big Blondy laughed. Then he grinned at the old man, and asked mockingly, "You recollect any of your killings yet, Blackie?"

Old Joey shivered and shook his head firmly. "Can't say I do. I try. But my mind won't go beyond the hospital!"

The big man laughed. "Well, seeing I'm leaving you right after the rain's cleared up and the going is easier, I got to tell you a big joke."

"A joke? Who on?" Joey eyed him curiously.

"On you, old-timer!" He leaned back against the cave wall and grinned at Joey. "Y'see, Joey, you ain't Blackie Sanders at all. You're just a poor old hobo that probably fell off a freight car and got a bad bump on the head. You ain't *anybody!*"

Old Joey looked startled. "But you recognized me—"

Blondy chuckled and waved it aside. "I'm a great kidder, old man. I was ribbing you."

"But, Blondy—" Joey was bewildered now.

The big man interrupted with a laugh. "The name is Sanders. And the front handle is Blackie."

Joey blinked at him, speechless. It was too much for him.

"There's no harm telling you now," the big man grinned. "I'll be pulling out real soon." Then he scowled suddenly and leaned close to Joey, gripping the front of Joey's shirt in one hairy hand. "But till I do, you're going to stay real close at hand. Don't get any notions about running to the law. If you try to make a break, I'll forget my manners."

Uncle Petrie had lost no time getting Sheriff Bennett on the telephone from the Martin farm. Within a half hour, Bennett and two deputies had arrived to start the search for Letty.

Timmy stood watching, with Lassie beside him, as the men piled into the official-looking car.

Ruth called, "Good luck!" but Timmy suddenly made

up his mind and ran to the side of the car.

"I bet Lassie could find her! Do you want us to go along?" he asked eagerly.

"No, Timmy," Carl Bennett said quickly, "but thanks just the same. I'm sure we can find her without Lassie."

Timmy stood watching the car drive off, and he patted Lassie's head. "They weren't very polite to you," he told her solemnly, "but *I* know you could find her easy."

Ruth saw his expression, and she called out cheerfully, "Why don't you go on over to see Boomer? You haven't played with him for days!"

Timmy hesitated. He thought he would like to see Boomer all right, but Boomer might still be mad at him.

"I have to phone his mother about something else. Shall I tell her you're coming over?" Ruth asked brightly. She thought that Timmy was worrying about Letty, and it would do him good to be with Boomer till Letty was safely home with her folks.

"I guess so." Timmy wasn't enthusiastic. "Come on, Lassie." He went to get his bike, and a few minutes later Ruth saw him ride off along the muddy main road toward the Bates farm, with Lassie running by his side.

She felt relieved. Now Timmy wouldn't take it into his

head to tag along after the men.

But it didn't work out the way she expected.

Boomer had forgotten all about being snubbed at the Martin home. He was glad to see his pal Timmy, and excited when Timmy told him of Letty's disappearance.

"I told Sheriff Bennett Lassie could find her," Timmy complained, stroking Lassie, "but he didn't believe me."

"Hey! Why don't we just go anyhow, and let Lassie look for her? We know a lot of places in the dark part of the woods that the sheriff doesn't know, I betcha!"

"Yeah!" Timmy's eyes sparkled, "and if we don't find her right off, we can go talk to Joey, and ask if he's seen anybody around!"

"Let's go!" Boomer ran into the shed and wheeled out his bike. "We can ride part way, till the brush gets too thick. And look!" He pulled a small whistle out of his pocket and showed it to Timmy. He gave a couple of shrill toots on it. "If we get far apart, I'll whistle and you can come where *I* am."

That being agreed on, they set off briskly, pedaling as hard as they could, uphill and down. And in a very short time, they were well into the woods.

Lassie watched them dismount and hide their bikes under

the bushes. She sniffed the air inquiringly, as they didn't seem to know which direction to start toward.

A faint, tiny sound of barking came to her keen ears, and she sat up, whining softly.

Now the boys could hear it, too. "It's Pom-Pom!" Timmy shouted. "Come on! I bet Letty's with him!"

He led the way, crashing through the brush, in the direction of the faint barking, but Lassie pushed ahead of him after a few yards, in her usual protective position. If any danger should be ahead, she would meet it first.

When they came in sight of Pom-Pom, the puppy was balancing dizzily on a fallen tree trunk out in the middle of the rushing creek. The poor little animal was so wet that its usually fluffy coat was clinging tightly to its plump body, and its frantic little barks were turning into wails of terror, as its tiny nails slipped on the wet wood.

Just as they came in sight of it, the puppy gave a despairing howl, slipped off the trunk, and was carried roughly downstream. It disappeared in the turbulent water.

The boys stared helplessly after it, but Lassie didn't waste a second. She plunged into the rushing water, and let herself be carried downstream.

She kept her head up and watched the water closely for

a glimpse of the puppy, as she was borne along. For just a second, a small white body was tossed out of the water, as the current swerved around the foot of a rock. A second, but it was enough for Lassie!

She struck out with all her strength toward the spot where the puppy had appeared, and the boys, watching helplessly, saw her disappear into the water for a moment and then emerge, carrying a white bundle in her teeth.

They ran along the shore, and met her as she struggled up the muddy bank with the soaking wet, limp puppy. She stretched out, panting, as Timmy and Boomer gave the puppy first aid.

It took only a couple of minutes of massaging and pumping water out and breath into the tiny body, before the puppy gave a faint, protesting yip at the rough treatment.

"He's okay!" Boomer exclaimed triumphantly.

Timmy nodded. The puppy staggered to its feet, and went weaving over to Lassie. Then he crawled between her outstretched paws, curled up, and gave every sign that he intended to stay in that friendly haven. And Lassie licked the wet, cold little body in the gentlest way, till the puppy had stopped shivering and was asleep.

"I thought Letty'd be with Pom-Pom," Timmy sighed.

"Maybe he was lookin' for her, too. Same as us an' the sheriff," Boomer suggested.

Timmy pointed to some marks in the mud and sand at the edge of the path along the creek. "Hey! That looks like Taffy's hoofprints!" he told Boomer.

Boomer went over to look, and stepped on the same soft and treacherous piece of ground that Taffy had struggled against. "Yipe!" he yelled, waving his arms and grabbing at a bush to keep himself from sliding down the bank into the fast-moving water.

And as Timmy dashed over to lend a hand, he saw something familiar lying on the ground a couple of feet from the soft edge. He stopped abruptly, staring.

It was one of Letty's riding gloves.

"Gimme a hand!" Boomer was hanging onto that bush for dear life, and any moment he might have to let go and fall into the water—while his best friend stopped to gawk at something! "Hurry up!"

But, instead, Timmy picked up the glove, and stood staring at it with a dazed look on his face. "It's hers, all right!" he told himself. "She an' Taffy must've fallen in, about here. An' Taffy got out an' ran home—" he stared out into the rushing water as if he expected to see Letty

there, and then finished in a whisper as the full meaning
of the evidence struck him suddenly, "—but—I guess she—
she's still there . . . ."

Boomer had managed to catch hold of another, higher
bush with his free hand, and was valiantly hauling himself
out. He yelled crossly at Timmy, "Help me, won't you?"
but Timmy was standing looking out at the creek with a
strange expression on his face, and didn't seem to hear him
at all.

Boomer was almost up to dry ground, on the slippery
bank. Then as he tugged at the higher bush, its roots gave
'way, and he started to slide backward down the bank. He
gave a terrified yell.

Lassie got up quickly, but carefully so she wouldn't dis-
turb the round ball of white fur sleeping between her
paws. And when she had backed off from the puppy, she
trotted over to the very edge of the bank above Boomer,
leaned over and grabbed him by the back of his sweater.
Then, bracing herself, she started backing away and at
the same time hauling Boomer up, an inch at a time.

It was hard on the sweater, but it held Boomer from
dropping down into the swirling water. He yelled angrily
at Timmy, "Hurry up! What's the matter with you?" as

he tried to help Lassie help him. And Timmy snapped out of his daze enough to run over at last, and pull him up the final couple of feet to safety.

When Boomer was sure that he was really safe, he yelled tearfully at Timmy, "Why didn't you come when I called? I mighta drowned!"

Timmy looked at him wide-eyed, and showed him Letty's glove. "I found this in the mud. I guess maybe Letty was riding Taffy when he fell into the water."

Boomer's ruddy face was several shades paler as he stared at the glove, and then looked quickly out at the turbulent creek waters. "Maybe she could swim. Maybe she's okay."

Timmy shook his head solemnly. "She couldn't swim. Her dad was going to teach her"—his voice broke—"this summer!"

Lassie barked suddenly. She had heard something that they hadn't heard yet. She stood facing the road and barking excitedly.

"Maybe it's Letty! Maybe she did get out okay! Hey, Letty! It's us! Me an' Boomer!" Timmy yelled excitedly.

"Where are you?" Boomer shrieked. Then he remembered the whistle, and gave several shrill blasts on it. If she was anywhere within half a mile, she would hear *that!*

But it wasn't Letty who answered the whistle. It was Paul Martin. He ran toward them through the brush, with Uncle Petrie and one of the deputies at his heels.

"Timmy! Boomer! What are you doing here?" He frowned, looking around quickly for Letty. "Have you found Letty?"

"No, sir," Timmy answered sadly, "but we found this." He handed over the glove. "It's hers."

"And there's Taffy's hoofprints. That's where he fell into the water!" Boomer pointed. "I near fell in, myself, just now. I woulda drowned if Lassie hadn't held onto me, I bet!"

The three men exchanged quick looks as they examined the slippery bank. The pony could have slipped . . . the saddle could have twisted . . . and Letty could have been thrown into the flooding creek . . . .

"Boys, I think you'd better take Lassie on home now," Paul told them, trying to keep his voice light. "We don't want to worry your mothers. And Boomer needs some dry clothes anyhow."

"But Lassie can help you find Letty!" Timmy argued.

"Timmy!" Paul said sternly. "Do as I say! And get started right away."

The puppy was staggering around sleepily. "One of you had better carry that pup!" Uncle Petrie suggested. "Here, I'll show you how!"

He made a carrying sling of Timmy's jacket and tied it around Timmy's neck, hanging down in front. The puppy snuggled down quite comfortably in it, with only his small fluffy white head and his bright little eyes visible.

The two boys trudged off, much against their wishes.

Lassie, as usual, led the way as they went through the woods toward the road. But every now and again she stopped and gazed back in the direction they had come.

"See?" Timmy pouted. "Lassie doesn't want to go home! Her feelin's are hurt because Dad wouldn't let her help find Letty!"

"I bet they'd all feel silly if we did find her!" Boomer said bitterly. Then his eyes widened. "Say, why don't we do like you said, and go ask old Joey if he's seen her?"

"But Dad said to go home!" Timmy always tried to be obedient, even if it was a strain.

"Oh, okay!" Boomer looked scornful, "but it wouldn't take long to get to the cave, if we started right now. Then if Joey says he hasn't seen her, we can go straight home."

Timmy squirmed. "But it looks like she fell in the creek.

I could tell Dad thinks so, too, the way he got rid of us!"

"Well, s'pose she did fall in!" Boomer scowled. "That don't mean she couldn't climb out again some place along the creek, does it? 'Specially if she wasn't hurt much."

"Yeah!" Timmy looked happy for the first time in hours.

"Well? How about it?" Boomer still wanted to make the decisions and be the hero.

"Okay. Let's go!" Timmy agreed. And they started off hastily by a very faint trail that was their special short cut through the thick woods to the cave.

Sheriff Bennett and his other deputy had crisscrossed the woods, and were starting for the brush-filled ravines beyond, when they heard the single pistol shot that told them that Paul and the others had found something. They doubled back to a meeting beside the creek.

"It looks bad, at that," Sheriff Bennett agreed grimly, after examining the evidence of the hoofprints and the lost glove. "I'm afraid that when we do find her . . . ." He didn't need to finish it. The men could do that for themselves, unhappily!

They set out to search the creek banks as far as the first bend, a mile downstream. Things often washed ashore there, after a storm.

20

HOME AGAIN

Letty had been napping, curled up in the shade of the big sun-dappled rock. At first, she had cried a little about being lost and hungry, but the sun-warmed breeze had soon lulled her to sleep.

She hadn't felt brave enough to try to find her way home out of the big dark woods. Besides, she was afraid she might see the big man with the dead rabbits over his shoulder. He looked like a story-book ogre!

A distant revolver shot made her stir, and then suddenly she was wide awake. Something had touched her, and even now was nudging her shoulder. She was almost too scared to look, but then she heard a familiar little whimper, and she knew that a friend had found her.

It was Lassie, watching her with bright brown eyes, and now, putting a slim paw on her lap in greeting.

"Oh, Lassie! I'm so glad to see you!" Letty squeezed her so hard with both arms that Lassie hardly had enough breath left to bark. But she managed somehow! And she kept on barking.

A hundred feet away on the other side of a thicket, Timmy and Boomer were pushing along on their trail to the cave when they heard Lassie barking.

Timmy stopped abruptly. "Hey! She's found something! And she sounds like it's something she likes!"

Pom-Pom, riding peacefully up to now in the coat sling that Uncle Petrie had fixed up, seemed to hear something good, too, in Lassie's barking. He struggled to get out of the sling, and before Timmy could stop him he had leaped to the ground and run off in the direction of the barking. His own shrill yipping as he ran answered the deep wroofing of Lassie.

"Come on! Let's see!" Timmy yelled to Boomer, and immediately plunged into the bushes to follow the poodle. Boomer was close on his heels.

When Timmy came crashing through the brush, he was

astonished and delighted to see Letty, looking quite calm and serene on her rock, one arm around Lassie and the other around Pom-Pom, who was doing his best to tell Letty in his usual wildly enthusiastic way that he was delighted to see her again.

"Hi, Letty!" Timmy shouted. "We been lookin' all over for you! Are you okay?"

Boomer followed Timmy through the brush. "Hey, we thought you got drowned!"

Letty reassured them both, and then, after looking them both over eagerly, asked, "Didn't you bring along something to eat? I'm awfully hungry!"

"Eat?" They exchanged baffled looks. They hadn't thought about eating. They suddenly realized that they were hungry, themselves.

Then Timmy had a bright idea. "Maybe Joey has something to eat at the cave. We're only a little ways from there, and he'll be glad to give you some of his food!"

"Joey?" She frowned. "Who's that?"

"A nice old man, a friend of mine," Timmy explained.

Letty asked abruptly, "Does he have a black beard—an' big, big feet? An' does he shoot rabbits?"

The boys looked startled. "He has a beard, but it's gray,"

Timmy told her. "I never noticed his feet. But he wouldn't shoot a rabbit for anything, I know. He loves them, and they're all friends of his!"

Letty let out her breath in a sigh of relief. "That's good. Let's go."

Boomer frowned. "Whatcha wanta know about his feet for?"

Letty showed them the footprints that the black-bearded stranger had left when he passed earlier.

When she had finished telling them about him, Timmy said positively, "That wasn't Joey. He's real nice."

So they started off, three hungry ones. Lassie led the procession, with Pom-Pom frisking at her heels.

But their reception at the cave was to be anything but the friendly one that Timmy and Boomer were expecting.

For the last hour, the real Blackie Sanders had been sleeping. He had gorged himself on the rabbit stew, and then packed what was left of it into old Joey's cooking tin. "This I take along," he had told Joey.

"But it's all I got for cooking," Joey protested.

Blackie laughed harshly. "Seeing there ain't much here to cook, hobo, that don't seem to make much difference."

The news that this black-bearded, mean-eyed man was

the real escaped convict, and that *he* was still the nameless wanderer, had brought a measure of relief to old Joey. But if he wasn't Sanders, who was he? Just a homeless tramp, going nowhere? But where, then, was the hospital that he was so sure he could remember, even if all the rest was a blank? And why had he been there?

He was puzzling unhappily over his problem, when he heard Timmy's voice calling, "Mister Joey!"

He stole a quick look toward the corner where Blackie was sleeping. The big man hadn't moved.

Joey started moving hastily toward the cave mouth. He would send Timmy away, before Blackie could wake up and maybe frighten the boy.

But he was only halfway to the entrance of the cave, when Blackie snarled, "Hold it, hobo!" and Joey saw that he had risen and was striding toward him.

Joey wanted to run out and away, but the look in the black-beard's eye stopped him. He explained lamely, "It's one of the little kids. I'll chase him away. He might tell his pa there's two of us here now, if he saw you."

Blackie grinned crookedly. "Yeah, and *you* just might be figuring to slip him the word who the other guy is!"

"I won't tell him, honest!" Joey protested.

"I know you won't!" the big man snarled. "Because I don't figure to let you!"

"Joey! Yoo-hoo! Are you in there?" Timmy was calling, and Boomer's voice added, "Aw, I bet he ran away a long time ago! He was just a tramp!"

"He was not!" Timmy's voice was shrill. "He was my friend. An' I'm going in an' look for him. Maybe he's sick!"

"Okay, chase 'em away!" Blackie snapped. "But don't try to give 'em any messages. I'll be watching!" He patted the gun in his belt. "Play it cool!"

"I'm coming," Joey called out, a little shakily.

"He *is* there!" Timmy's voice shouted.

Joey was still a few feet inside the cave, when his foot struck the cartridge box that Blackie had stolen from Sam Moss's store in Calverton. It was empty now, and Blackie had discarded it. Joey scowled at it and gave it a kick ahead of him and out into the sunlight.

At sight of him, Timmy and Boomer started to hurry toward the mouth of the cave, with Letty a close third. But Lassie held back. The hair on the back of her neck stood up, and she growled as she stared at the cave.

Joey stopped the boys as they scrambled toward him. "Don't come in here!" he called out, trying to make it as

harsh as he could. "I don't want you young'uns hanging around here any more. You git! And don't come back!"

Timmy was astonished. He could hardly believe his ears. His friendly old man was scowling and motioning for them to go. "Hey, it's *us!*" he called out weakly to Joey.

Boomer's face got red, and he glared defiantly at Joey. "We don't have to go if we don't wanta!" he said sassily. "It was our cave first, an' *you* better move out, or I'll tell the sheriff!"

"Scoot! Get away from here!" Joey shouted. "I ain't leaving here! Tell anybody you like!" and he shook a threatening fist at them.

"Yah!" Boomer made a face. "Ol' tramp!" He held his ground impudently. "Who's afraid of you?"

But Timmy and Letty were not so bold. "Let's go back," Timmy said. "Come on." He tugged at Boomer's sleeve.

Lassie, who had put herself between Timmy and old Joey, growled and showed her teeth, but she didn't jump at Joey. And then Timmy noticed that she was looking past Joey and snarling at something deep in the cave.

"Git, I say!" Joey picked up the empty cartridge box and flung it toward them.

The empty box struck Boomer on the arm, and fell to the

ground at his feet. Angrily, he picked it up and was about to throw it back at the old man, when they all heard a loud sneeze from inside the cave. Boomer's arm dropped to his side, but he still unconsciously held onto the empty shell box. "Hey, what was that?" he asked Timmy, with a puzzled frown. "Sounded like a sneeze!"

Timmy thought so, too. Lassie was still staring at something in the cave that was bothering her—and Timmy felt pretty sure that whatever it was, it had sneezed. And it was a man-sized sneeze! He said hastily, "Let's get outa here!" and with that, he grabbed Letty's arm, and started hurrying her away from the cave. "Come on, Boomer!"

Boomer hesitated only an instant, then he turned and fled after them, almost tripping over Pom-Pom, who was racing after Timmy and Letty and barking gaily.

Lassie was the only one who held her ground, snarling past Joey at the man in the dark recess of the cave. She was Timmy's rear guard now, and she wouldn't move till he called her to come.

"Shoo, Lassie!" Joey waved his arm at her urgently. But she waited until, to Joey's relief, she heard Timmy call from a distance, "Come, Lassie! Lassie!" Then she backed a few steps watchfully, wheeled, and ran off.

Joey was shaking as he went back into the cave. "I drove 'em off," he told Sanders sullenly.

Then he busied himself cleaning up, puttering in the back of the cave. He felt sure Sanders hadn't noticed him throw the stolen cartridge box at the boy. Now, if the boy would do as he said, and go to the sheriff, they might come looking—

Almost as if he had read Joey's mind, Sanders said, suddenly, "I'm pulling out by sundown. Too many people around all of a sudden."

Timmy and Boomer helped Letty through the tangled brush, and the two dogs followed. But Letty was too tired to go far. "You go on," she told the boys bravely.

"Nothin' doin'," Timmy said fiercely. "We're not leaving you!" Then he sat down to wait for her to rest, much to Boomer's annoyance. Boomer wanted to get out of there.

Lassie suddenly started barking loudly. A moment later, they heard Paul Martin shouting in answer, "Timmy! Lassie! Where are you?"

Then all three yelled at once. A few minutes later, Paul Martin, Uncle Petrie, and several others, found them.

Sheriff Bennett and Paul were so delighted to see Letty safe and well, that they didn't pay much attention to the excited report from the boys, about the stranger in the cave.

But all of a sudden, Sam Moss noticed the cartridge box in Boomer's hand, and recognized it as the one that had been stolen from him. He showed it to the others excitedly.

"Where is this cave?" Paul asked Timmy.

"We'll show you," Timmy volunteered, but Boomer didn't want to go back there. He wanted to go home. He had had enough excitement for one day.

"Timmy, you and Lassie can lead us, while Uncle Petrie takes Letty and Boomer home," Paul suggested.

That suited everyone, and Uncle Petrie was soon on his way, carrying Letty on his shoulder, and with Pom-Pom and Boomer tagging after.

When they got in sight of the cave, Paul told Timmy to stay back, in case of trouble with Joey and his unknown companion. But Timmy was worried about old Joey, and he tagged along, with Lassie, against orders.

There were three of them, Sheriff Bennett, Paul, and Sam Moss, as they went cautiously toward the dark mouth of the cave. They were making as little noise as possible, but Blackie Sanders had already heard them, and was waiting just inside the cave, gun in hand.

The first man within range would be his target.

Joey saw them coming, and knew what was going to happen. At the last moment, he flung himself at Blackie's gunhand, and tried to disarm the convict.

But Blackie had expected something like that, and he knocked the old man away from him with a powerful blow of his fist. Joey staggered and collapsed in the dirt.

The men outside, hearing the struggle, rushed forward, and Blackie turned his revolver toward them. Paul Martin was in the lead, moving fast. In another second he would be in easy range. Blackie cocked his revolver, but as he did, something struck his arm.

It was Lassie, a snarling, growling bundle of fury.

Before Blackie could get over his surprise and turn the revolver on her, she had knocked him down, and had fastened her teeth in his wrist, pulling and tearing at it till his fingers relaxed. He dropped the gun and yowled.

Paul ran forward, swept up the gun, and leveled it at the convict. He called off Lassie. "All right, girl! We've got him now!" he told her.

The handcuffs were soon on Sanders' wrists. He was angry and defiant. "You never woulda had a chance," he boasted, "if that goofy old guy hadn't jumped me. And this cur—" He glared at Lassie, who curled her lip up over her teeth and glared back. Blackie decided to say no more!

"Mister Joey!" Timmy ran into the cave. Then they heard him yell, "Dad! Mr. Bennett! Please come quick!"

They found him kneeling beside the unconscious Joey. "Please do somethin' for Joey!" he pleaded. "He's hurt!"

The men stared down at the gray-bearded stranger. "He looks sort of familiar," Sam Moss said, frowning.

Joey was starting to come to, now. Timmy and Paul leaned over him. "Mister Joey! Are you all right?" Timmy asked anxiously.

And as Paul helped the old man to sit up, he looked at them with surprise. "Who—who are you? Where am I?"

Suddenly Sam Moss remembered. "Joe Brunson!" He leaned over. "Joe! It's me, Sam Moss! And you're home in Calverton!"

Recognition dawned in Joey's eyes. "Sam! What's been going on? How did I get here?"

That was a question that was answered within a few days. Joe Brunson had had a head injury during the war, and had lost his memory completely.

For several years he had drifted from one government hospital to another, taking treatments, but failing to remember anything of his past. Then one day he had run away, and instinctively had drifted to the old valley where he, his wife, and his boy had spent a few happy years.

Letty was proud and delighted to have a grandfather, and Dave to have a father again. Dave's only regret was that they would still have to give up the farm. Several people wanted to buy it, and even with his father's farming ability, they would have to sell it to live.

But they were due for a happy surprise the very day before they had planned to move.

Thanks to the testimony of those who were at the taking of Sanders, the reward for his capture went to Joe Brunson, who in addition had undoubtedly saved Paul Martin's life by his reckless attack on the armed convict.

The reward money would enable them to stay on at the farm, and be happy. And it also gave them a chance to do something to show Timmy how much they appreciated Lassie's help through it all.

The something was a wonderful leather collar, with a metal tag on it. The engraving on the tag said, TO LASSIE, THE BRAVEST EVER.

And from the way Lassie strutted when she wore it, Timmy almost decided that maybe she *could* read. It seemed quite possible, considering everything else she had done!

Whitman
CLASSICS

Five Little Peppers Midway

Mrs. Wiggs of the
Cabbage Patch

Fifty Famous Fairy Tales

Eight Cousins

Little Women

Black Beauty

Five Little Peppers and
How They Grew

Treasure Island

Heidi

The Call of the Wild

Tom Sawyer

Beautiful Joe

Adventures of Sherlock Holmes

Little Lame Prince

Here are some of the best-loved stories of all time.
Delightful... intriguing... never-to-be-forgotten
tales that you will read again and again. Start
your own home library of WHITMAN CLASSICS
so that you'll always have exciting books at your
finger tips.

Whitman ADVENTURE and MYSTERY Books

Adventure Stories for GIRLS and BOYS...

TIMBER TRAIL RIDERS
The Long Trail North
The Texas Tenderfoot
The Luck of Black Diamond
Mystery of the Hollywood Horse
The Mysterious Dude

POWER BOYS SERIES
The Haunted Skyscraper
The Flying Skeleton

DONNA PARKER
In Hollywood
At Cherrydale
Special Agent
On Her Own
A Spring to Remember
Mystery at Arawak
Takes a Giant Step

TROY NESBIT SERIES
Sand Dune Pony
Diamond Cave Mystery
Indian Mummy Mystery
Mystery at Rustlers' Fort

New Stories About Your Television Favorites...

Dr. Kildare
    Assigned to Trouble
    The Magic Key

Janet Lennon at Camp Calamity

Walt Disney's Annette
    Mystery at Smugglers' Cove
    Desert Inn Mystery
    Sierra Summer
    Mystery at Moonstone Bay
    Mystery at Medicine Wheel

Combat! The Counterattack

The Beverly Hillbillies

Lassie
    Secret of the Summer
    Forbidden Valley
    Mystery at Blackberry Bog

Lucy and the Madcap Mystery

Patty Duke and Mystery Mansion